D0055093

WINGS
OF
FIRE

THE WINGLETS QUARTET

WINGS OF FIRE

THE WINGLETS QUARTET
THE FIRST FOUR STORIES

by
TUI T. SUTHERLAND

SCHOLASTIC PRESS
NEW YORK

Compilation copyright © 2020 by Tui T. Sutherland
Map and border design © 2012 by Mike Schley
Illustrations © 2012 by Joy Ang

All rights reserved. Published by Scholastic Inc.,
Publishers since 1920. SCHOLASTIC and associated logos are trademarks and/or registered trademarks of Scholastic Inc.

The publisher does not have any control over and does not assume any responsibility for author or third-party websites or their content.

No part of this publication may be reproduced, stored in a retrieval system, or transmitted in any form or by any means, electronic, mechanical, photocopying, recording, or otherwise, without written permission of the publisher. For information regarding permission, write to Scholastic Inc., Attention: Permissions Department, 557 Broadway, New York, NY 10012. Adaptations from Wings of Fire: *Winglets #1: Prisoners* © 2015 by Tui T. Sutherland; Wings of Fire: *Winglets #2: Assassin* © 2015 by Tui T. Sutherland; Wings of Fire: *Winglets #3: Deserter* © 2016 by Tui T. Sutherland; and Wings of Fire: *Winglets #4: Runaway* © 2016 by Tui T. Sutherland.

This book is a work of fiction. Names, characters, places, and incidents are either the product of the author's imagination or are used fictitiously, and any resemblance to actual persons, living or dead, business establishments, events, or locales is entirely coincidental.

ISBN 978-1-338-73239-9

10 9 8 7 6 5 4 3 2 1   20 21 22 23 24

Printed in the U.S.A. 40
This edition first printing 2020

Book design by Phil Falco

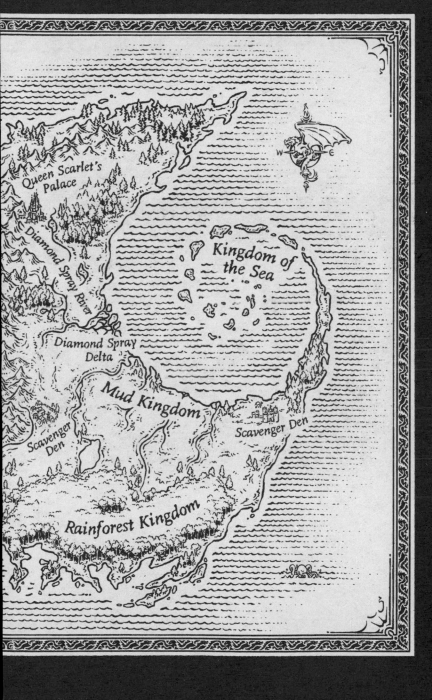

Ice Kingdom

Kingdom

A NIGHTWING GUIDE TO THE
DRAGONS

Sand

Scorpion Den

Jade Mountain

Queen Scarlet's
Palace

Dia

m of
a

W

OF PYRRHIA

Scavenger
Den

Scavenger

Rainforest Kingdom

~ SANDWINGS ~

Description: pale gold or white scales the color of desert sand; poisonous barbed tail; forked black tongues

Abilities: can survive a long time without water, poison enemies with the tips of their tails like scorpions, bury themselves for camouflage in the desert sand, breathe fire

Queen: Since the death of Queen Oasis, the tribe is split between three rivals for the throne: sisters Burn, Blister, and Blaze.

Alliances: Burn fights alongside SkyWings and MudWings; Blister is allied with the SeaWings; and Blaze has the support of most SandWings as well as an alliance with the IceWings.

MUDWINGS

Description: thick, armored brown scales, sometimes with amber and gold underscales; large, flat heads with nostrils on top of the snout

Abilities: can breathe fire (if warm enough), hold their breath for up to an hour, blend into large mud puddles; usually very strong

Queen: Queen Moorhen

Alliances: currently allied with Burn and the SkyWings in the great war

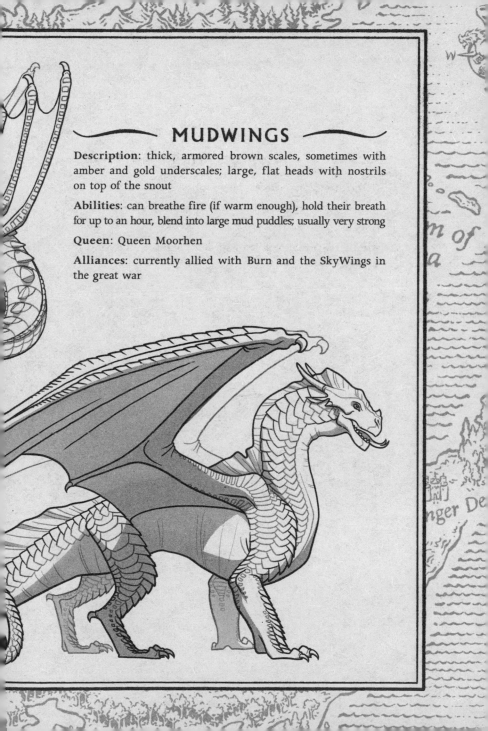

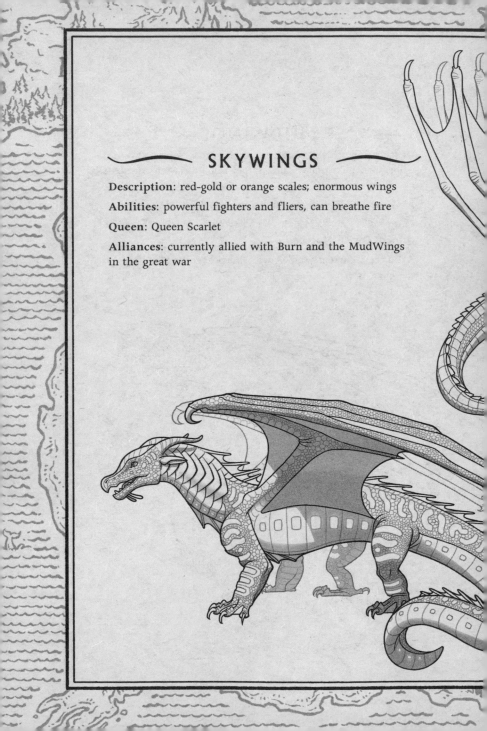

SKYWINGS

Description: red-gold or orange scales; enormous wings

Abilities: powerful fighters and fliers, can breathe fire

Queen: Queen Scarlet

Alliances: currently allied with Burn and the MudWings in the great war

SEAWINGS

Description: blue or green or aquamarine scales; webs between their claws; gills on their necks; glow-in-the-dark stripes on their tails/snouts/underbellies

Abilities: can breathe underwater, see in the dark, create huge waves with one splash of their powerful tails; excellent swimmers

Queen: Queen Coral

Alliances: currently allied with Blister in the great war

ICEWINGS

Description: silvery scales like the moon or pale blue like ice; ridged claws to grip the ice; forked blue tongues; tails narrow to a whip-thin end

Abilities: can withstand subzero temperatures and bright light, exhale a deadly freezing breath

Queen: Queen Glacier
Alliances: currently allied with Blaze and most of the SandWings in the great war

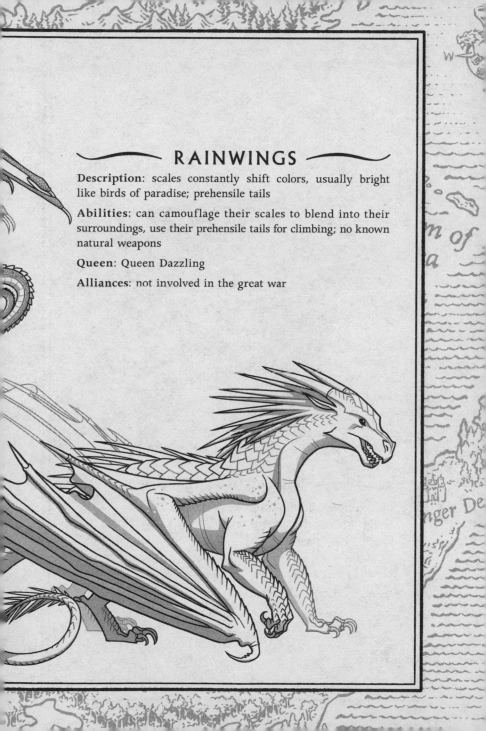

～ RAINWINGS ～

Description: scales constantly shift colors, usually bright like birds of paradise; prehensile tails

Abilities: can camouflage their scales to blend into their surroundings, use their prehensile tails for climbing; no known natural weapons

Queen: Queen Dazzling

Alliances: not involved in the great war

NIGHTWINGS

Description: purplish-black scales and scattered silver scales on the underside of their wings, like a night sky full of stars; forked black tongues

Abilities: can breathe fire, disappear into dark shadows, read minds, foretell the future

Queen: a closely guarded secret

Alliances: too mysterious and powerful to be part of the war

THE DRAGONET PROPHECY

When the war has lasted twenty years . . .
the dragonets will come.
When the land is soaked in blood and tears . . .
the dragonets will come.

Find the SeaWing egg of deepest blue.
Wings of night shall come to you.
The largest egg in mountain high
will give to you the wings of sky.
For wings of earth, search through the mud
for an egg the color of dragon blood.
And hidden alone from the rival queens,
the SandWing egg awaits unseen.

Of three queens who blister and blaze and burn,
two shall die and one shall learn
if she bows to a fate that is stronger and higher,
she'll have the power of wings of fire.

Five eggs to hatch on brightest night,
five dragons born to end the fight.
Darkness will rise to bring the light.
The dragonets are coming. . . .

WINGS OF FIRE

OF

FIRE

WINGLETS #1: PRISONERS

Note: Contains spoilers for Wings of Fire
Book Five: *The Brightest Night*

This is Pyrrhia, where there are seven dragon tribes.

There were seven queens.

Then came a great war, a prophecy, a volcano . . . and after the War of SandWing Succession was over, a shift in the balance of power.

Not everyone approves of the new SandWing queen.

In fact, the only topic more controversial is the new queen of the NightWings.

Can they hold on to their thrones?

Should they?

In the dungeon of the SandWing stronghold, two prisoners await . . . what? A trial? Imminent execution?

They're not exactly sure.

They are NightWings, but they cannot go back to their tribe. They are in exile; they are too dangerous to be allowed to return. And yet: too complicated to be killed. (They hope.)

So they wait, and scheme (well, one of them schemes. The other one is catching up on sleeping and eating). And they wonder what will happen to them.

All they want is access to the most dangerous weapon of all:
a chance to tell their own story.

They are prisoners.

But perhaps that is about to change.

For the guard with the scar over her heart:

I've been watching you. You're not like the other guards — the bowing, scraping, mindlessly loyal lizards who live for your queen. You have your own thoughts, don't you? You're smarter than the average SandWing. And I think I know your secret.

Let's talk about it.

Third cell down, the one with two NightWings in it. I'm the one who doesn't snore.

I HAVE NO INTEREST IN DISCUSSING ANYTHING WITH A NIGHTWING PRISONER.

WHOSE IDEA WAS IT TO LET YOU HAVE PAPER AND INK?

You *should* be interested. You're going to need allies for what you're planning . . . and when I get out of here, I'm going to be a very useful ally indeed.

—•—

AMUSING ASSUMPTIONS. MY QUEEN BELIEVES YOU'RE GOING TO BE IN HERE FOR A LONG, LONG TIME.

—•—

True . . . but she also believes she's going to be queen for a long, long time . . . doesn't she.

—•—

An interesting silence after my last note. Perhaps it would reassure you to know I set your notes on fire as soon as I've read them. You can tell me anything, my new, venomous-tailed friend. Believe me, Night-Wings are exceptionally skilled at keeping secrets.

—•—

WE ARE NOT FRIENDS.

I DON'T KNOW ANYTHING ABOUT YOU, OTHER THAN WHAT IT SAYS IN YOUR PRISONER FILE.

FIERCETEETH: TRAITOR. KIDNAPPER. RINGLEADER OF ASSASSINATION PLOT.

TO BE HELD INDEFINITELY WITH FELLOW TRAITOR STRONGWINGS, ON BEHALF OF THE NIGHTWING QUEEN.

OH, YES, CERTAINLY SOUNDS LIKE A DRAGON ANYONE CAN TRUST.

She's not my queen. You can't be a traitor to someone who shouldn't be ruling over you in the first place.

Which might be a thought you've had lately yourself, isn't it? I know some things about you, even without a file.

Saguaro: Prison guard. Schemer. Connected to great secret plans.

We're not so different, you and I. Particularly when it comes to trustworthiness.

Just think, if my alleged "assassination plot" had worked, the NightWings would have a different queen right now. Perhaps it would even be me.

Well, if at first you don't succeed . . .

I could tell you my story, if you get me more paper to write on.

Or you could stop by one midnight and listen to it instead. But I've noticed you don't like spending too much time in the dungeon. Is it the *tip-tap* of little scorpion claws scrabbling everywhere? The stench rising from the holes in the floor? The gibbering mad SandWing a few cages down who never shuts up, all night long? (What is her story? Has she really been here since the rule of Queen Oasis?)

Or is it that you can too easily picture yourself behind these bars . . . and you know how close you are to joining us?

◆●◆

ALL RIGHT, NightWing, here's a blank scroll. Go ahead and try to convince me that you're a dragon who even deserves to live, let alone one I should waste my time on.
I do enjoy being amused.

◆●◆

THE DRAGONET WITH NO DESTINY
(According to Certain Other Idiots, not According to Her)

I hatched on an island of smoke and fire, under a volcano that breathed death all day and hid the stars and the three moons at night.

My tribe was dying. There were fewer eggs every year, and even fewer of those survived to become dragonets, and all of those were starving, along with everyone else.

NightWings keep their secrets well. None of the other tribes suspected what was happening to us. None of them even knew where we lived.

But they knew about our powers of mind reading and seeing the future.

And that was what was going to save us.

A prophecy. THE prophecy.

That *stupid*, claw-scraping, moonsbegotten prophecy.

Every dragon on Pyrrhia probably knows it by heart (unless you're an ignorant RainWing). Or at least they've heard the important verse: *"Five eggs to hatch on brightest night, five dragons born to end the fight. Darkness will rise to bring the light. The dragonets are coming. . . ."*

And everyone knows it's about five ever-so-special dragons who were destined to stop the war and save the world. If you've met them, though, you might have noticed that they're not all THAT special. They're kind of sappy and disappointing, don't you think? Especially the NightWing. He's a walking tragedy.

You know why?

Because it should have been *me*. I would have been perfect for the prophecy. I would be *brilliant* at saving the world. I would also have been brilliant at leading the other dragonets, proving that NightWings are the best tribe, and making sure things happened exactly as we wanted them to.

Just one problem: I didn't hatch on the brightest night.

I hatched two years too early.

STUPID SNIVELING MOONS IN THE WRONG PLACE AT THE WRONG TIME.

And so you know who got to be the all-special chosen NightWing instead? My little brother. HOW UNFAIR IS THAT?

I was even *there* when his magical destiny landed on him. I was standing right next to his annoying egg in our hatchery, talking to our mother. Her black scales gleamed in the firelight as she curled around it, brushing the eggshell lightly with her claws.

"Take me hunting," I wheedled. I don't wheedle anymore, just for the record. "Please? I need help. I keep losing my prey after I bite it, and I think other dragons are eating it before I find it again."

So we're clear, I didn't *really* need help. I mean, I was as hungry as everyone, but I can take care of myself. What I wanted was for Mother to stop being drippy and boring and for her to leave that egg alone for even half a second.

"I can't, little one." Mother sighed one of her long, scale-rippling sighs that made her tail flop over. "What if something happens to my egg while I'm gone? It's so close to hatching now."

"What could happen?" I demanded. "Do you think it's going to roll away? Sprout wings and fly off the island? Turn blue and pop out a SeaWing instead? It'll be fine, and you *staring* at it all the time isn't going to make *any difference.*"

She fixed her black eyes on it as if to prove me wrong. "This might be the only time I get to spend with it," she whispered. "The brightest night is coming. . . ."

"Blah blah BLAH!" I shouted. "This might be the only time you get with *me*, too! I could get *exploded by a volcano* tomorrow!"

She winced. "That's not going to happen," she said. "Mastermind says we have a few more years before another explosion is due."

"HA," I said. "I bet I get blown up before you take me to the mainland. Remember all those promises you made? Or I should say, all those lies you told me?"

"Fierceteeth, you're only two years old," she said. "You'll get to the mainland one day. And when your little sibling hatches we'll have plenty of time together as a family."

"YUCK!" I shouted. "That doesn't count! I don't want a drooling dragonet following us around!"

No one else I knew had to put up with this — this *competition* for their parents' attention. Yes, yes, it was unusual, Mother was special, let's all clasp our talons and coo in awe.

Here's why: Most NightWings don't have two eggs. Thanks to our horrible death trap island home, most NightWings haven't been able to have even *one* egg in the last . . . I'm not sure, but it's been a really long time. My friend Mightyclaws is the only other dragonet I know with a sibling right now.

But I didn't see why Mother *needed* another egg when she had *me*. It should have been exciting *enough* that *I* was hatched. I mean, it *used* to be.

And then suddenly she was all "EEEE, another egg is coming, life is SOOOO wonderful" and wasn't she proud of herself and obsessed with it. It was like she completely forgot about her first perfectly wonderful egg and the perfectly wonderful dragonet that came out of it.

I think it was stupid Morrowseer's fault. (If you don't know who he is, count yourself lucky.) He was losing his mind around then, yelling at everyone all the time; you did *not* want to stand between him and any lava, just in case. See, Morrowseer was trying to make sure someone had eggs that would hatch at least *near* the brightest night. He really wanted some choices for his glorious prophecy.

Instead, he got only one egg with the right timing. One blah little egg that was the center of Mother's universe.

So Mother had just told me no, she couldn't leave her precious boring second egg to take me hunting, and I was sitting there glaring at it and wondering who I could trick into cracking it for me. It was small for a dragon egg, and black, the color of our scales, so it basically looked like an extra lump sticking off Mother's tail.

And then we heard the THUMP-THUMP-THUMP of grumpy talons stomping our way, and in comes gigantic Morrowseer, all frowning and portentous as usual.

"I've come for your egg, Farsight," he said to Mother. That's Morrowseer — not exactly a "good morning, how are you, nice grim sulfur-smelling weather we're having" kind of dragon. But then, neither am I, so I can respect that.

Mother clutched the egg closer to her. "Mine?" she said. "Are you sure?"

Morrowseer waved his wings impatiently at the nearly empty hatchery. "Do you *see* a hundred other options somewhere?" he barked. He jabbed one claw toward the only other egg in the cave. "That one isn't due to hatch until after the brightest night. Yours is it. Congratulations, you're the mother of a prophesized dragonet. Now hand over that egg."

"But . . . right now? Won't I get to meet my dragonet?" Farsight asked. "Can't we let the egg hatch here and give it to the Talons of Peace later? She could grow up with us, and then we could send her to the continent in a few years. Wouldn't that be better, to raise her like a real NightWing?"

(Mother was doing that dragon thing of assuming her special perfect egg had a female dragonet inside. WRONG.)

Morrowseer snorted. "Unnecessary. Our genetic superiority will manifest wherever this dragonet hatches and however it is raised. And the Talons need to *think* they're in charge of the dragonets, at least for now."

Mother looked down at the obsidian black egg between her talons. "Will my dragonet ever come back?" she asked.

"Listen, you're not the mother I would have chosen either," Morrowseer snapped. "I'd have picked someone who knew who the father was, for one thing." (Note: It wasn't MY father. My father died before I hatched, according to Mother. Starflight's father was someone else, but Farsight either couldn't or wouldn't say who.)

Morrowseer went on: "It should have been someone with more backbone and less fluff between her ears. Like Secretkeeper; she's got a sensible head on her shoulders and she'd hand over her dragonet for a prophecy in a heartbeat. But she hasn't got a dragonet, and you do, so do your duty and give it to me." He lowered his voice to a growl. "For the sake of the tribe's *survival*, Farsight."

I didn't quite understand all that back then, of course. NightWing secrets are handed out bit by bit to dragonets as we get older. I'd heard of the Talons of Peace, but all I knew was that they were an underground movement trying to end the War of SandWing Succession.

But here's what I did understand: Morrowseer was taking that egg someplace far away from the island. The dragonet in that egg was going to grow up in a world with proper trees and sky and plenty to eat. The Talons of Peace would treat it like a queen, and one day it would save the entire NightWing tribe.

"You could take me instead," I blurted. "I can fulfill the prophecy! I don't have *any* fluff between my ears!"

Morrowseer barely glanced at me. "You're much too old," he sniffed.

"So send me out later and lie about my age," I suggested. "How would anyone know when I was hatched? I'm scrawny enough. A year from now I bet I could pass for a one-year-old."

"Fierceteeth, stop," my mother whispered.

"She's bold," Morrowseer said, flicking his gaze over me for a moment longer. "Boldness is useful. Idiocy, however, is not." He reached out and snatched the egg from Mother's claws. She let it go without protesting any more, although she gave it the most soppy, cow-eyed, woeful look you've ever seen. It made me want to claw her snout right off.

"Thank you for your service to the tribe," Morrowseer snarled at her. He turned to stomp away.

"Think about my offer!" I called after him. "Bad things happen to little dragonets all the time! If you need a backup prophecy dragon, I'll be right here!"

He paused in the cave entrance, a shudder rippling down his spine. For a long moment he didn't move, and then he turned his head slightly, just far enough to give the last remaining egg a dark, thoughtful look. And then off he went, with the egg that turned out to contain my brother, Starflight, the *least* bold and *most* idiotic NightWing who has *ever hatched in the history of Pyrrhia*.

Was I thrilled that my competition was gone? Did I welcome my mother back with open wings, ready to be her precious beloved one and only again?

I most certainly did not. I wasn't going to be duped anymore. Now I knew how easily she could drop me. I'd seen how shallow her loyalty ran.

Maybe if she had begged my forgiveness . . .

But she didn't. Instead she MOPED for AGES and it was SO BORING, you have no idea.

So I spent my time and energy on Morrowseer instead. He was the one with useful connections. He was the one who could get me to the continent and maybe into that prophecy, once he realized how completely NightWing I am.

(That's another word for awesome, if you're slow on the uptake, SandWing.)

I followed him around the fortress. I showed up whenever he was lecturing, even if it wasn't to my class. I happened to be around whenever he needed a message sent to someone. I "accidentally" ran into him in the island's small patch of forest and "coincidentally" drove prey in his direction.

In my head, I sometimes pretended he was my father.

But did all that work make him like me even one tiny bit?

Not as far as I could tell.

And did he ever send me to the mainland?

NOT ONCE.

Technically, NightWing dragonets aren't allowed off the

island until they are ten. Apparently we need ten years of training in how to keep the tribe's secrets first.

But I was GREAT at keeping secrets, and if my dopey BROTHER could be on the mainland all that time, I didn't see why I couldn't at least *visit* it. Especially once the tunnel to the rainforest was built. It would have been so easy to let me hop through some night when no one was around. I just wanted to breathe real air and see the stars for a *minute*. That didn't seem like too much to ask — and I did ask, over and over again, until Morrowseer called me a pest and banished me to the dragonet dormitory.

My point is that I grew up in the most terrible place in Pyrrhia, but it made me strong. This dungeon is nothing in comparison. Here, we get to eat every day and your queen even lets us out to stretch our wings more frequently than I can believe.

But I deserve to be free. Everything I did, all my so-called "crimes," were for the good of my fellow NightWings. I was trying to find us an ally who would restore our power. I was trying to save us from being controlled by another tribe. I was trying to make sure we had a real home of our own!

And if I had succeeded, *I'd* be the hero right now, instead of those bleeding heart "dragonets of destiny."

I *deserve* to be part of my tribe again, and they deserve a queen who cares about them and understands what they've suffered — not the teeth-grinding mistake they have now.

I believe in the separation of the tribes and the importance of maintaining the royal bloodlines, if possible. I suspect you do, too.

One way or another, I'm getting out of here. If you help me, you'll gain a determined ally who can help you get what *you* want.

If you don't, you'll be just another guard I have to kill on my way out.

— *Fierceteeth*

I SEE. QUITE A TRAGIC TALE.

WHAT ABOUT YOUR FELLOW PRISONER? THE ACCESSORY
TO YOUR CRIMES?

IS HE A MISUNDERSTOOD HERO AS WELL? IS HE NECESSARY
TO YOUR AMBITIOUS PLANS, OR DO YOU INTEND TO LEAVE
HIM HERE TO DESICCATE?

Strongwings is coming with me wherever I go. Forever. That's non-negotiable.

I don't care if no one understands why he's mine. It's my heart; I can stick whomever I want in there.

But I'll tell you some of his story since it is late and I cannot sleep at night anymore, not when there's moonlight pouring in through those small, high-up windows. Also, I enjoy wasting the queen's lamp oil.

And if you are even considering setting me free while keeping him trapped, I will roast your talons one claw at a time.

(Or perhaps I'll simply betray you to that six-clawed interrogator who oversees the guards — I bet *he'd* like to hear about the secret map you've been drawing of the stronghold, or the way you stand in dark corners and whisper to someone who isn't there.)

I knew Strongwings from the moment I hatched, although I did not particularly like him at first. He was three years older than me, but the dragonet dormitory in the NightWing fortress had more than enough space for the smattering of dragonets in the tribe, so we all lived there together until the age of ten.

Strongwings was a notorious mess and possibly the slowest dragon in the tribe. He kept leaving bits of carcasses around his sleeping spot, or accidentally stepping on everyone's tails on his way to bed at night. He never spoke in class, unless it was to say something boneheaded to one of the other dragonets, who always ignored him. Everyone ignored him. *I* ignored him. I was too busy and ambitious to make friends. Besides, he wasn't the sharpest claw on the dragon, if you know what I mean.

I only remember feeling mildly relieved when he turned ten and was moved to the adult quarters, taking his mess and his snoring and his stupid jokes with him. I didn't even see him again until a few months later, soon after my seventh hatching day.

It was a miserable day on the island — more miserable than usual, I mean. The clouds were pouring this drippy mix of rain and sleet all over us, so it was cold and wet outside but stifling inside, and all the ashes in the air were sticking damply to our wings and creeping into our snouts, so it felt as though we were breathing volcano even more than usual.

I snuck out of class because I couldn't take one more minute of Great and Glorious NightWing History when my lungs felt like moldering sacks of wet paper. That teacher is nearly blind anyway; he didn't even notice me slipping out the back tunnel.

The halls of the fortress smelled like wet dragon. Gusts of damp wind and splatters of sleet kept swirling in through the cracks in our walls, sizzling on the coals and turning the air smoky. I was looking for somewhere as far away from the outside as possible — a corner of the fortress that was completely protected — and I thought of Mastermind's lab.

Mastermind was our science teacher, and the tribe's resident genius, if you can believe all the hype about him. I say, if he's such a genius, he should be able to explain stuff in a way that dragons can actually understand. Instead he showed up once a week, blathered on for hours using the biggest, most made-up words possible, and then slithered back to his lab, leaving all of us even dumber than we were before.

He had a whole giant inner room of the fortress for his experiments, and it was well protected from the outside air. Mastermind was obsessive about keeping other dragons from touching his stuff, but maybe I could sit in a corner and . . . hmm. Well, maybe he wouldn't be there.

He was definitely there.

"YOU'VE RUINED IT! THE WHOLE THING! OUR ENTIRE TRIBE COULD BE WIPED OUT BECAUSE OF YOUR STUPIDITY!"

I paused outside the door that said LABS and tilted my head, listening. There was an enormous crash and then several smaller crashes. And then scrabbling talons, and I just barely managed to leap back before the door slammed open and a beefy black dragon came charging out, flapping his wings wildly.

"AND DON'T COME BACK OR I WILL DISSECT YOU ALIVE!" Mastermind's voice bellowed as the door swung shut.

The dragon flopped over on the floor, panting for breath.

"Hello, Strongwings," I said. "Causing disasters as usual, I see."

"Oh," he said, sitting up fast. "Uh, hi, Fierceteeth."

"What did you do now?" I asked.

"I knocked a bottle of . . . uh . . . something into a vat of . . . uh . . . something else," he said. He scratched his head, looking mournful. "There were bubbles . . . and some weird gas . . . I don't know. Sometimes he explains the experiments to me, but that just makes it more confusing."

"Kind of an idiot MudWing move, going in there in the first place," I observed. "You plus breakable things and unstable chemical compounds? Clearly a bad idea."

"That's what I said!" he protested. "I didn't want this job! It was Mother's idea, and she's friends with Princess Greatness, so that's, you know, they made it happen. But I told them the dumbest NightWing ever hatched shouldn't be Mastermind's assistant."

There were a few more ominous crashing sounds from behind the door.

I realized Strongwings was giving me a funny look.

"What?" I demanded.

"I was kind of hoping you'd disagree with me there," he said.

"About what?" I asked.

"About me being the dumbest NightWing who ever hatched."

"Oh," I said. "Sorry. I *would* have, if I could think of anyone dumber."

He actually laughed, which was intriguing. Most NightWings will try to counter your sarcasm with more sarcasm, as though every conversation is a competition to see whose wit is more biting. No one ever stops to acknowledge that someone else is funny.

"Ah well," he said. "Perhaps they're right. I'll probably be less trouble here than crashing around leaving 'obvious trails' in the rainforest."

"You've been to the rainforest?" I narrowed my eyes at him. "What was it like? Tell me everything at once."

He glanced at the door to the lab, then bared his teeth at me in an awkward way, which turned out to be his version of a smile. "Or I could just show you."

"That's not funny," I snapped. "I may be half your size, but I can still bite you."

"I'm serious!" he protested. "I can distract the guard and take you through. No one will find out, and if they do, what are they going to do to me? Give me a worse job than this? Pretty sure there isn't one."

I could think of much worse punishments I'd personally witnessed — things involving lava or an extra week between rations — but I didn't bring them up. If this crazy dragon wanted to take me to the rainforest, I wasn't going to talk him out of it.

"Fine. We should find out who's guarding the tunnel," I said, striding off down the hall.

"Oh, uh — right now?" he said. "I mean, uh . . . yes, right now. Of course. That is when we are going. Now. Yes, that's what I meant."

I ignored his mumbling. I have found that all interactions work better when you only pay attention to the things that are actually said to you, instead of the things you think they're trying to say.

"Should be Deadlyclaws today, I think," he said, catching up to me.

"He's quite sharp," I said. "What's your plan?"

"Um . . ." he said.

I glared at him. "You DO have a plan."

"I do! I do. I got it. Don't worry."

He paced along beside me, flicking his wings and furrowing his brow. I'd never stood this close to him before, but now it struck me that he really was nearly twice my size. He was unusually burly for a starving NightWing — you could still see his ribs, but they were big ribs, attached to a big back and massive shoulders. He could probably grow to be even bigger than Morrowseer one day.

I liked that thought. I liked walking down the hall next to, essentially, a small lumbering mountain. It kind of made me feel as if I had something that would shield me from the lava if the volcano *did* explode all of a sudden.

We left the fortress and flew over the molten landscape in the rain. My wings were instantly soaked and chilled to the bone, but I didn't care. We were going to the tunnel. We were going to the *rainforest*. I'd hovered outside the cave before, but I'd never been in. No dragonets anywhere near the secret tunnel, that was the rule.

Did I care about breaking it? No, I did not. It was a stupid rule. One that could apply to other dragonets, but not to me. I was at *least* as clever and trustworthy as Mr. Fatwings over here. Besides, the nice thing about doing it this way was that *he'd* get in trouble, not me.

Well, so I thought, anyway.

"Uh . . . wait here," he said, steering us down to the beach. My talons sank into the wet black sand and I squinted through the downpour as he flew up to the cave. A few moments later, he appeared at the entrance and waved to me.

That was weird. I hadn't seen Deadlyclaws come out.

Turns out, that's because Strongwings's idea of a "distraction" was to sneak up and clonk someone over the head. Deadlyclaws was lying unconscious inside the cave, next to a small fire in front of the tunnel entrance.

I regarded him for a moment.

"He won't wake up for a while," Strongwings mumbled.

"I see," I said. "Did he see you?"

"Uh," he said. "No? I don't think so. He was poking the fire."

Well, it would be idiocy to waste this opportunity. I climbed over Deadlyclaws and stepped into the tunnel.

"Hang on," Strongwings protested. "*I'm* taking you to the rainforest. That means I go first. Scooch over."

I snorted a small flame at him, spread my wings, and flew into the darkness with him flapping along, grumbling, behind me.

Up and up, around and sideways, and then — the chill fell out of the air, and light shone up ahead.

I burst out into sunlight.

And warmth.

And *breathing*.

You can't understand it because you grew up with all of that. Most dragons don't spend a single moment of their lives thinking about breathing, but for NightWings, it's an ongoing, horrible experience. On the volcano, you suck in particles of ash with every breath. Your lungs always feel like they're on fire. The inside of your throat is scraped like you've been swallowing giant pieces of eggshell.

I guess we're used to the smell of sulfur and rotting prey and smoke, but once you leave it — once you notice it — it's *awful* to go back to.

Stepping into the rainforest was like plunging my snout into a cauldron full of plants. I was so overwhelmed by the assault on my nose that I didn't even register what was in front of my eyes for the first few minutes.

I just breathed. And smelled. And smelled and breathed and *breathed*.

At last I was able to focus on Strongwings's face, his black eyes peering into mine, a wild assault of greenery erupting behind him.

"You look enormously pleased with yourself," I said sharply.

"I knew this would do it," he said, tucking his wings in with a self-satisfied nod. "I've never ever seen you smile, but I knew if I brought you here . . ."

I glared at him. "Does that make you some kind of genius? I'm sure every dragon reacts the same way."

Now my senses were adjusting and I could also hear the sounds of the rainforest: the rushing wind in the trees, the chatter of golden-furred monkeys overhead; the faraway calls of birds, the nearby river burbling contentedly to itself. I could feel the humming heat of the sun melting into my scales.

"Yes, that's true," Strongwings said, "but I wanted to be the one to see *your* face."

I studied him suspiciously. "Why?"

"Because —" He floundered, his claws stabbing nervously at the dirt below us. "Uh. Because you're — well, you're just — you're the only Fierceteeth. You know?"

That was true. I AM the only Fierceteeth. I don't need doting parents to tell me I'm special and brilliant and ferocious. I don't need a prophecy to make me unique and important. I am FIERCETEETH.

But it was unusual for someone else to notice.

"Hmm," I said, taking a step closer so I could eye him up and down. He did not appear to be joking or teasing me. In general I am not a fan of sentimental sincerity — in general that is *not* a NightWing trait — but it turns out there are certain dragons who can pull it off.

Well, one. There is *one* dragon who can talk to me like that without getting bitten, or stabbed, or bitten AND stabbed.

"Want to go flying?" he asked. "And eat mangoes? And jump in a pool of water that is not cold gray sludge, or so full of salt that all your scratches burn like fire?"

I did want to do all those things. But I had never pictured doing them with Strongwings, of all dragons. I didn't want him to think I was a dragon who would just lower all my defenses the moment I felt sunshine on my scales.

"Oh, right," I scoffed. "As if *you* are fast enough to catch a *mango*. I'd like to see *that*."

He started laughing again, although I wasn't entirely sure why this time. Dragons who might be laughing at me usually have an unpleasant encounter with my claws before they draw their next breath. But for some reason his laughter didn't make me want to stab him in the nose.

So we flew, and we swam, and we ate more food than I knew existed in the world, and I did not care even one tiny iota when we returned to the tunnel hours later, as the sun was slanting down through the trees, and found glowering Morrowseer and furious Deadlyclaws waiting for us.

I decided to go on the offensive before they could start yelling.

"Oh, good. I have something to say to you, you conniving, lying snake," I snapped at Morrowseer as we landed. Strongwings jumped and sidled a step away from me, then two steps closer to me. I could feel his gaze melting along the side of my face — shocked, or anxious, or impressed; I didn't know which and couldn't be bothered with him right then.

"Do you know how many rules you've broken?" Morrowseer bellowed, ready to launch into his prepared rant. "How dare you — *what* did you just say to me?"

"I called you a conniving, lying *snake*," I spat. "Why can't we move here right now? Why would you keep us on that miserable island a moment longer when *this* is *here*, ready and waiting for us?" I spread my wings at the forest around me.

"Don't question your elders," Morrowseer fumed. "You have no idea what the risks are, or what else must be done —"

"What risks?" I shot back. "The RainWings? Are you afraid they're going to throw bananas at you? It would probably take them months to even notice we're here."

This was before we discovered what RainWings could do, obviously. It wasn't in any of the scrolls. We didn't find out until about a year later, when a dragon called Vengeance got a demonstration all over his stupid face. (No big loss, for the record. He was hideous before the encounter with that RainWing, too.)

"It's Queen Battlewinner's decision," said Morrowseer,

"and she has decided we're not ready. Would you like to take it up with her?"

That shut me up for a minute. No one had seen the queen in years, but she spoke through Morrowseer and her daughter, and in the fortress we could feel her eyes on us all the time. She knew everything, and if you were unlucky enough to catch her wrathful attention, her punishments were always swift and severe.

"And don't forget the IceWings, you arrogant dragonet," Deadlyclaws growled. "If we saunter in and make our home here, how long will it be before they find out where we are? We're safe on the island, but once they find us here, they'll swoop down to kill us all."

"That's right," Morrowseer hissed. "The queen's plan will give us the powerful ally we need to protect us in our new home. So we stick to the path of the prophecy. That's the only way for us to do this safely."

"And you could have jeopardized all of it," Deadlyclaws added. "You could have been seen without even realizing it. A camouflaged RainWing could have spotted you and be reporting back to their queen right now."

"Or what if you had been captured?" Morrowseer snarled.

"Captured by RainWings?" I rolled my eyes. "Terrifying."

"You'll be sorry for this," he hissed. "I'll make sure you never set claws in this rainforest again, not until we move here."

No one was going to see my despair, I told myself fiercely. *Don't let him know that it feels like your eyes are being ripped* out. *Don't let him see that you care.* I curled my claws into the ground as if I could root myself there, so no one could ever drag me away. Quietly I inhaled, trying to drag the scent of mangoes and moss and river rocks deep into my lungs, trying to imprint this place on my scales forever.

"But it's my fault," Strongwings blurted suddenly. "This was my idea, not hers."

"Ha!" Morrowseer shot a blast of smoke out of his nostrils. "Fierceteeth has been badgering us about coming here for years. We know what she's like. There's no need to take the fall for her . . . whatever your name is."

"I'm telling the truth," he insisted stoutly. "I told her I'd bring her here. *I* knocked out Deadlyclaws — sorry about that."

Deadlyclaws snarled at him.

"She wouldn't be here if it weren't for me," he said. "Punish me instead."

He *was* telling the truth, but he didn't have to. I had already decided not to shove the blame onto him. And clearly Morrowseer had decided what he wanted to believe, too, based on what he already thought of me.

"So you're suggesting we ban *you* from the rainforest instead?" Morrowseer said mockingly.

"Yes," said Strongwings.

"Don't be an idiot," I said at the same time. "I wasn't supposed to see this place for three more years anyway. You're old enough to get put on hunting duty or assigned to a spy mission here. Don't throw that away for nothing."

"You're not nothing," Strongwings said with an odd catch in his voice.

And maybe his slowness had infected me for the day, too, because that's when I finally figured it out.

The risk he'd taken wasn't about proving his bigness or enjoying a daring trip outside the rules. For Strongwings, this was about *me*.

He saw me, and had seen me for a while, although I'd never noticed before.

Unlike certain other dragons, if Strongwings was given a choice, he would choose *me*.

I wrapped my tail around his and lifted my chin dcfiantly at Morrowseer. "You can punish us together," I said. "We don't care."

And he did, by the way, but it wasn't anything worse than regular life on the island. We had some terrible extra assignments for a year, but we did them together, which made them less terrible. And we figured out a smarter way to sneak off to the rainforest without getting caught. (Well, *I* figured it out and let him come along.)

Anyway, that's a long story to illustrate a simple point: Strongwings is my dragon. He will do anything to keep me alive. He is the only dragon I trust in all of Pyrrhia.

And I am not going anywhere without him. Put that up your snout and smoke it.

— *Fierceteeth*

YOU ARE A COMPLICATED DRAGON, NIGHTWING.
SUPPOSE I COULD HELP YOU, AS YOU PRESUME.
WHAT IS IT, EXACTLY, THAT YOU THINK YOU CAN
DO FOR ME?

HOW IT SHOULD HAVE BEEN

All right, Saguaro, SandWing guard with a scar over your heart. This is basic logic, so it shouldn't strain your brain too much to follow along.

Imagine for a moment that my plan had succeeded.

Imagine that I had talked my companions into going to the stronghold instead of stopping for help in the Scorpion Den. (Their idea, and a terrible one, as I should have guessed it would be.)

Imagine that I had ended up in Burn's throne room instead of in prison.

Now picture me giving her on a silver platter exactly what she wanted: the location of the prophecy dragonets.

Can you see it in your mind? The army of SandWings en route to the rainforest? With me and Burn flying in the lead, like the avenging wings of night and day swooping down to set history right?

Who could have stopped us? The RainWings are no warriors; they would have rolled over and begged for mercy the moment they saw a SandWing's claws. The other NightWings would have joined me in a heartbeat.

And then they would have helped Burn in return . . . so what would the world look like now, if my plan had worked?

Queen Burn of the SandWings.

Queen Fierceteeth of the NightWings.

The prophecy: fulfilled the *right* way. The dragonets: all dead — such a sad story, but sacrifice is what happens to heroes, right?

(Well . . . maybe not *all* dead. I'd show mercy to my little brother, even though he betrayed us. No need to waste a NightWing. I'm sure he could be rehabilitated eventually.)

And I really would have saved my tribe — *me*, the dragonet with no destiny. *I'd* be the hero, after all that.

But the dream's not dead, my friend. We can still make this happen, even if it's with a slightly different cast of characters.

Listen, you're clearly a smart dragon . . . well, let's say smartish. I bet you supported Queen Burn. And I also bet you have someone else in mind for the throne now. From the way you've been skulking around, taking notes and studying everything, I bet you're quite the useful inside dragon for somebody.

So be even more useful. Give yourself and your secret plan some allies that can really help you.

It's very simple. We don't like our queen. You don't like your queen. Together we eliminate them, and then our tribes can go back to ignoring each other forever.

But first you have to get us out of here.

As soon as possible, please. I'm getting sick of smelling SandWings and eating dried camel every day.

— *Fierceteeth*

—◆●◆—

Did you read my letter? Why haven't you responded?

—◆●◆—

Saguaro, I am not a patient dragon. If you do not help us escape, I will tell someone what you've been up to. To be blunt: I'm sure the current SandWing queen would be *very* interested to hear about the mysterious spy among her guards.

—◆●◆—

VERY WELL, YOU MADDENING NIGHTWING. YOUR STORY HAS WARMED MY HEART, OR PERHAPS I JUST NEED YOU TO GO AWAY AND STOP SLIDING INCRIMINATING NOTES UNDER YOUR DOOR.

SO.

MIDNIGHT TOMORROW.

BE READY.

WINGS OF FIRE

OF

FIRE

WINGLETS #2: ASSASSIN

Note: This story is set approximately
two years before the brightest night when
the prophecy dragonets hatch.

Deathbringer was a dragonet who followed orders.

Read this scroll, sweep this cave, catch that exact fish, kill that misbehaving prisoner — whatever it was, he did it, no questions asked.

(Well. He'd wanted to ask questions about the prisoner. Such as: Why did anyone bring a mud dragon to the secret night dragon home in the first place? Of course he would have to die; no one could know where they lived. And why make a four-year-old dragonet kill him? There were plenty of NightWing guards who would have been happy to take that order instead. But that was his assignment, and so of course he did it, as cleanly and quickly as he could.)

Obedience to your elders: the most important thing a young NightWing had to learn. That, plus loyalty to the tribe and how to keep a secret.

But his new assignment was a bit . . . confusing.

"You want me to spy on the queen?" Deathbringer tilted his head at Quickstrike, the dragon who had taught him everything he knew. "*Our* queen?"

"If she's there," Quickstrike answered. "I'll be meeting with Greatness in an hour in the council chamber, and I want you to sneak in and listen, if you can."

He wasn't quite sure how to feel about this order. It rather confused his idea of who was in charge of him.

On the other talon, Greatness wasn't really the queen; she was the queen's daughter and her mouthpiece. No one had seen Queen Battlewinner herself since she'd abruptly disappeared from public view several months before. Maybe she'd be there, hidden and listening, but maybe not.

And possibly this was a test that the queen actually knew about. Quickstrike always had bigger reasons behind her orders, even when they seemed mysterious. Besides, what else was he going to do: disobey her? Not likely; not ever.

"Be as stealthy as you can," Quickstrike said before turning away. "And meet me afterward at your sleeping cave."

Deathbringer headed straight for the council chamber, giving himself time to avoid any guards that might be posted. The shadows swallowed him up, black against black, and he kept his wings folded to hide the glittering spray of silver scales underneath.

He slipped through one of the back tunnels into the chamber that emerged directly below the Queen's Eye, and then slithered along the wall to the closest cave. There was no way to know if the queen was there, watching from behind her stone screen, but just in case, he stayed out of her line of sight. He tucked himself into the darkest recesses, feeling jagged rock press against his back and tail.

It felt like hours before he finally heard approaching talons. But this was something he'd worked on with Quickstrike, too: staying perfectly still, no matter how much his muscles screamed.

"There had better be a point to all this," growled a deep male voice. Deathbringer wasn't sure who that was.

"You don't have to be here," a female voice snapped. That one was easy; Deathbringer had been listening to Quickstrike's voice every day since he'd hatched, after all. "Greatness, this is a matter for you, me, and the queen. Nobody else."

"Morrowseer is one of the queen's most trusted advisors, and she wants him consulted on anything that might affect the prophecy," Greatness answered. She always sounded a little nervous, as if she wasn't sure anyone would believe anything she said.

"That's right," Morrowseer said smugly. "So what are you trying to get away with now, Quickstrike?"

"Wait," Greatness said. "Let me stand by the Queen's Eye, in case Mother has anything to say." The sound of her wings flapping filled the cave, and Deathbringer pictured her flying up to perch beside the screen. "All right," she called. "Go ahead."

"You know I'm being sent to the continent," Quickstrike said, plunging right in. "To carry out the council's new strategy of targeted assassinations, starting with the growing threat from the Kingdom of the Sea. I'm here because I want Deathbringer to be on my team."

It took all of Deathbringer's concentration to keep still. He hadn't realized this meeting was going to be about *him*.

The continent!

"No," Morrowseer growled. "Don't be absurd."

"*You* don't get to decide," Quickstrike snapped. "The queen is still the queen, despite all your pretensions lately, Morrowseer."

"It does go against all our rules," Greatness said apologetically. "He's just too young, Quickstrike. You know we never let dragonets leave the kingdom until they're ten years old. Isn't he only four?"

"Yes, but he's the smartest dragonet in the tribe," Quickstrike said. "And if we want to train him to be our next assassin, he needs to start now. He needs to know the geography of Pyrrhia and the way the seven tribes work. He needs to understand the politics of this war for the SandWing throne. He needs to learn how to slip into a tent and slice open an IceWing's throat without waking the rest of the army."

Deathbringer *knew* he could learn all of those things. He wanted to learn them *so badly*.

Please let me do this. Don't make me stay here for six more years instead.

He'd heard rumors about this new strategy. The other dragon tribes were locked in a vicious war, and it was up to the NightWings to make sure it went the right way. Assassinating specific targets was part one of the plan . . . but making sure no one ever found out the NightWings were involved was parts two, three, four, and five.

Secrecy: that was the NightWing watchword.

And also the reason for keeping dragonets away from the other tribes. The older dragons didn't trust anyone under ten to keep their mouths shut if they were ever captured by, say, the SkyWings or SandWings.

"He can't learn to be an efficient assassin from here," Quickstrike went on. "And if I die on this mission, you'll have no assassin, and no way to train another."

"Can't you train an older dragon?" Greatness said over Morrowseer's skeptical snort. "Choose someone who's already ten."

"Like Vengeance," Morrowseer suggested. "Or Slaughter. They would love to practice killing other dragons."

"Vengeance and Slaughter both have boulders for brains," said Quickstrike. "Deathbringer could stab out their eyes and tie their tails in knots before they even noticed he was on the same island as them. I want him and no one else. He can keep your secrets, even though he's young. And I'm not leaving him here to be trained by someone inferior to me."

"This has nothing to do with him being your son, I suppose," Morrowseer hissed.

"I don't treat him like a son," Quickstrike growled. "I treat him like a student. He's my apprentice. The council agreed to that when he hatched; that's why he's called Deathbringer. And he's lived up to the name. He'll be the greatest NightWing assassin of all time if you let me take him on this mission."

Please say yes, Deathbringer prayed. *Please please please say yes.*

"He's killed *one* MudWing prisoner," Morrowseer said. "That's hardly a prediction of future murderous greatness. Leave him with me and I'll make sure —"

"I would *never* leave him with you!" Quickstrike shrieked.

"Wait," Greatness called over the two dragons' shouting. "Stop! Shh! The queen is speaking."

Silence fell in the council chamber. Deathbringer had seen this before: Greatness leaning toward the Queen's Eye, listening intently to the voice only she could hear.

"The queen has a proposal," she said finally. "The dragonet must prove himself to be as good as you claim, Quickstrike. If he can kill either Vengeance or Slaughter tonight, in stealth, before the sun rises, then he can go with you. If not, then you must choose one or both of them instead."

There was a long pause.

Why is she hesitating? Deathbringer wondered. *Doesn't she know I can do this?*

"What if — what if one of them catches him and kills him?" Quickstrike asked, her voice suddenly much slower than usual.

"Then we'll know he was all wrong for this mission," Morrowseer said with a smug chuckle.

"Tonight," Greatness said. "This is his one chance, if you think he's really ready. Or if not, you can choose not to test him. Then you must leave him here when you fly to the continent tomorrow."

Tomorrow? Quickstrike was leaving so soon?

Deathbringer tightened his jaw muscles. *I'm going with her, no matter what it takes.*

◆●◆

The first step was finding Vengeance and Slaughter, which should have been easy after Quickstrike's training. One of Deathbringer's regular assignments was memorizing the new guard roster and the rotating hunting schedule every week. So he knew that Slaughter was supposed to be on watch, patrolling the outer towers, and Vengeance was not scheduled for hunting.

But he also knew these dragons, at least by reputation. They were cousins, both of them bad-tempered and mean to everyone except each other. Even from a distance, Deathbringer knew that Slaughter was lazy and Vengeance was greedy and disobedient.

He also knew that no one had been enforcing the guards' duties since Battlewinner's — disappearance? Retirement? Whatever she was doing behind those screens. Greatness was too overwhelmed, Morrowseer was focused on the prophecy, and most NightWings felt that patrolling and guarding were stupid, unnecessary tasks that no one should have to do.

After all, if none of the other tribes could *find* the NightWings, then what was there to guard against?

So probably the last place he'd find Slaughter was patrolling on the outer towers. And Vengeance could easily be slithering around hunting when he wasn't supposed to be.

But the most likely scenario? Was that they were both fast asleep.

Deathbringer considered finding his mother first — she'd left the council chamber with Greatness and Morrowseer. He knew she was expecting to meet him back at the dragonet sleeping caves. But he already knew his assignment, and he wanted to prove he could do it without her help. Midnight was fast approaching. There weren't many hours for him to complete his mission.

He closed his eyes and consulted the map in his head. Slaughter and Vengeance both slept in communal caves with other NightWings; he could find those easily, but it would be very difficult to kill them stealthily if other dragons were there.

Vengeance's cave was the closest — and Vengeance was in luck, because two dragons were playing a game with bones and tiny skulls in the entranceway. Deathbringer glanced in, acting casual, as he went by. He didn't think Vengeance was one of the three sleeping dragons in the far niches, but he had no way to make sure without drawing attention.

So, Slaughter's cave. Up a long, winding tunnel, past the library, past the throne room, down another tunnel.

The hall was empty. No sounds came from the yawning mouth of the cave ahead.

Deathbringer crept toward it on silent talons.

A faint sound made him freeze for a moment. It came again, and he realized it was a snore, but nothing like the giant snores he heard every night from Strongwings, the noisiest sleeper in the fortress. He waited a moment, then crept forward again until he could see into the cave.

Six sleeping dragons, their black wings rising and falling as they dreamed.

He slipped between them, studying their faces in the orange glow from the walls.

And there he was. Slaughter, fast asleep, drooling a little. He was too thin, like most NightWings, and had a twitchy, furious look, even in his sleep. Deathbringer remembered him from a training class in which Slaughter had injured a small dragonet by playing too rough and then bragged about it afterward.

He'd be no big loss to the tribe.

And yet — he was a NightWing. A dragon Deathbringer had actually spoken to. A member of his tribe.

The weight of the order suddenly hit Deathbringer like a cave collapsing. Could he really bring himself to kill a fellow NightWing? In his sleep, no less, like a coward?

Not like a coward. Like an assassin. Stealth is the whole point. This is what I've been training for.

The sleeping dragon let out a long sigh through his nose,

breathing smoke into Deathbringer's eyes. Deathbringer blinked until he could see clearly again, keeping the rest of his body as still as a stalactite.

If I don't do this, I'll be left alone here. His father was dead. He had no brothers or sisters. His mother could be gone on this mission for years, she'd said. *What will happen to my training? Will Morrowseer take over? What will he turn me into?*

I need to go with Quickstrike.

Not only that, but going with her would mean leaving the Night Kingdom, which was everyone's dream. The continent was safe (apart from the war), and clean (apart from the other dragons), and there was so much prey there that he'd be able to eat *every day.*

That's where his destiny was. The greatest assassin in Pyrrhia would never hesitate over a small matter like killing one of his own. The queen herself had ordered this.

His claws wavered in the air as he reached for Slaughter's throat.

He'd do it to me in a heartbeat. He wouldn't need a reason, just an order.

That's the real test: Can I follow orders? Will I do exactly as I'm told, no matter what it is?

I can. I will.

Slaughter was about to draw his last breath when suddenly there was a scraping noise from the hallway. Deathbringer pressed himself to the floor, out of sight of the entrance.

Heavy talons stepped into the room. Deathbringer could hear wingtips brushing the roof and the sound of a growl in the back of someone's throat.

He crept backward, away from the rocky niche where Slaughter slept, until he was hidden behind the next sleeping spot and the snoring dragon there.

But he could still see the top of the wings that approached Slaughter's bed, and he could hear the whispering voice that woke him.

"Slaughter," it hissed. "Wake up. Silently. Come with me."

Slaughter let out a long grumbling whine and then a muffled yelp as whoever it was wrapped strong claws around his snout.

"I said silently. Get up."

Scrambling noises followed. If Slaughter thought *that* was silent, then he *definitely* shouldn't be allowed on any stealth missions. *He'd probably get Quickstrike killed,* Deathbringer thought angrily.

"What's happening?" Slaughter whispered as the two dragons began to pad out of the cave.

"Someone is coming to kill you," the other dragon growled. "But we're going to prepare you to kill him first."

Morrowseer. Deathbringer had guessed it from the moment he heard the talonsteps. Morrowseer was sabotaging his chances of completing the mission. Fury gripped Deathbringer in its powerful claws.

Breathe through it. Don't get caught. Don't do anything fool-ish. Don't let your rage be the queen of you.

Don't let him win.

"Wow," Slaughter said, sounding a little more awake. "Great. I've been *asking* for someone to kill for *ages*."

Deathbringer waited until they were just outside the cave and then he glided after them, navigating the other sleeping dragons cautiously. He glanced around the corner and spotted Morrowseer leading Slaughter up the tunnel toward the throne room.

"Where is your cousin?" Morrowseer growled at Slaughter, who was still rubbing his eyes and making sleepy noises.

"How should I know?" Slaughter grumbled. "Sleeping? Like anyone would be?"

"No, he's not there," Morrowseer said.

"Then hunting, I guess," Slaughter said with a shrug.

"It's not his turn —" Morrowseer stopped with a hiss. "Yes. You're probably right." They reached the narrowest part of the tunnel, where dragons could only walk single file, and Morrowseer strode ahead, muttering furiously.

"Who's trying to kill me?" Slaughter asked. "Do I get to kill them with a spear or with my bare claws?"

Deathbringer darted along the wall until he was right behind Slaughter. In a pouch around his neck, deadly silver discs thumped against his chest. He'd only started training with them last week; normally he'd be more comfortable with his claws. But the discs were faster and quieter. He'd only have one shot to get this right. Carefully, he slipped one out and palmed it.

"A dragonet with an inflated sense of his own abilities," Morrowseer called back. "He's been told that he will be a great assassin one day, and the queen has decided —"

As the huge dragon kept speaking, Deathbringer leaped onto Slaughter's back, clamped his snout shut, and slid the serrated edge of the silver disc neatly from one ear to the other, across Slaughter's throat.

There was a soft bubbling sigh from the wound, and then a gentle thud as Deathbringer lowered Slaughter's head to the floor. Both were muffled by the echoing sound of Morrowseer's voice waxing on about impertinence.

By the time Morrowseer turned around, Slaughter was dead, and Deathbringer was gone.

—◆—

Quickstrike was pacing in front of the dragonet sleeping caves, her forehead furrowed with anxiety in a way Deathbringer had never seen before.

"Deathbringer!" she cried when he appeared from the shadows. "Where have you been? Why didn't you follow my orders?"

"I did," Deathbringer said, surprised. "I was there. I heard your whole meeting with the queen."

"You — but I didn't sense you there —" She eyed him with distrustful, glittering eyes. "Are you lying to me?"

"I wouldn't!" he said indignantly. "I hid myself well, just like you taught me. I was listening the whole time. You're leaving for the continent tomorrow and I'm going with you."

"No," she said. "You're not. You have to stay here."

"Not according to what I heard," he said. He held out his talons, still coated in Slaughter's blood. "See? Mission completed. We can leave at sunrise."

She stared down at his blood-soaked claws. "What — what did you —"

"Exactly what you've been training me for," he said. He'd expected a slightly more delighted reaction, he had to admit to himself. "Slaughter is dead. No thanks to Morrowseer, who tried to warn him, which is pretty rude, don't you think?"

"You did it?" she whispered. "You really killed Slaughter?"

He described the kill to her, the way she'd described her kills to him many times, using precise, swift language to capture the fight in as many heartbeats as it had taken to complete it.

"Why do you look so worried?" he asked when he finished. "I was following Queen Battlewinner's orders."

"I was going to tell you not to do it," she said, rubbing her forehead. "Because it was too dangerous."

"Oh," Deathbringer said. "But . . . it worked out so yay?"

"It's still dangerous," said Quickstrike. "Morrowseer will want to punish you. He won't be pleased that one of his pets is dead."

Deathbringer shrugged. "He agreed to the deal. He should have known what would happen."

"He could still cause trouble for us. Or he could force us to bring Vengeance along as well, who will hate you and try to hurt you for what you did to his cousin."

Deathbringer wasn't concerned. He knew he could take Vengeance as easily as Slaughter, even if both of them were more than twice his size.

Quickstrike thought for a brief moment, then sighed a curl of smoke. "There's only one thing we can do — leave right now," she said. "If it's already done, no one can stop us. Do you need anything?"

"No," Deathbringer said, feeling as if all his blood had been replaced with lightning. He could fly all the way to the sun if she told him to. "I'm ready. Let's go!"

Moments later, they were aloft. The Night Kingdom was fading away behind them, and Deathbringer's great future as an assassin was spread out before him like the sunrise.

→●→

Two weeks into their expedition, they paused on the east coast of Pyrrhia, a short flight north of the Diamond Spray Delta. Here the forest crowded up toward the ocean, leaving only a strip of pebbled beach populated by arrogant seagulls and befuddled seals.

"Our first target is a SeaWing." Quickstrike spread her wings for balance as waves lapped the rock below her.

In two weeks of training and scouting, so far no NightWings had found them. Deathbringer kept dreaming of black wings descending from the sky, with talons clutching a scroll that commanded his return so he could be punished for murder.

He wasn't quite sure where these nightmares came from. During the day, he didn't worry about that at all. He knew he'd followed his queen's orders. He'd earned his place on this mission.

And it was *glorious* to be here, flying through snowy mountains and thick forests and over the beautiful sea. They'd avoided all other dragons carefully — NightWings weren't supposed to be seen, if they could help it — so mostly they'd been keeping to untouched parts of the continent, full of prey that could be caught and eaten as easily as picking fruit. Quickstrike had been running new training exercises with him every day, under blue skies, in wind that smelled like a million possibilities.

Deathbringer had never been so happy. If NightWings came to take him back, he thought sometimes that he just wouldn't go. He'd run off and live alone in the forests instead.

Not really, of course. He'd follow orders, as he always had. But if they couldn't ever *find* him to *give* him those orders, that would be fine by him.

"What SeaWing?" he asked, circling over her head.

"First, tell me who they're allied with," Quickstrike ordered.

Deathbringer landed on the beach, not far from the boulder where she was perched. He started writing in the sand with one claw.

"There are three sisters who want the empty SandWing throne," he recited. "The oldest, Burn, who has control of the main SandWing stronghold. At the moment, she's got the SkyWings on her side, probably by offering them territory along the Great Five-Tail River.

"Next, Blister, the smartest sister. She's allied with the SeaWings and the MudWings, and nobody knows where her base or her SandWing followers are.

"Finally, Blaze, the youngest and reportedly not the sharpest claw on the dragon. She's hiding with the IceWings, but slowly winning support from SandWings who have fled the desert due to Burn's cruelty."

"That's right," Quickstrike said. "As of now, Blister is the most powerful, to the point where we are worried that she could win the war in the next few months. She's smart and devious and pays her soldiers very well, and her allies cover a vast swath of territory. We need to slow her down."

"Because we don't want her to win," Deathbringer said.

"Because we don't want *anyone* to win for another ten years," said Quickstrike, her black eyes glittering.

"I see," said Deathbringer, watching a pair of green crabs march obliviously across his claws. "So our mission is to drag out the war."

"There's a plan in place," said Quickstrike. The wind buffeted her wings and she dug her claws into the rock. "Every piece of it must work in order to ensure the future of the NightWing tribe. This is our piece, and it starts with Commander Tempest."

"The SeaWing," said Deathbringer. "Our target."

"Yes. Blister has found a military ally as smart as she is, but even more fearless. In the last few months, Commander Tempest has led forays into SkyWing and SandWing territory that have been devastating for Burn's army. Between her and Blister, they could win this war."

"But they won't," Deathbringer said confidently. He sank his talons into the sand, spreading his wings to feel the sea breeze. "We'll stop them."

"It's not that easy." Quickstrike shook her head. "The SeaWings have two palaces — the Summer Palace and the Deep Palace — but no one knows where either of those are, and they're probably underwater. You're very talented, but I haven't noticed you sprout gills lately."

"What if we kill Blister instead?" Deathbringer suggested. "She must be out on land somewhere, right?"

"*Absolutely not,*" Quickstrike snapped with sudden ferocity. "You must not kill any of the three queens! It would ruin everything! Leave them alive *at all costs*, do you understand?"

Deathbringer blinked up at her. He didn't understand at all — but he could see that he wasn't supposed to. He was supposed to follow orders and let the plan unfold according to someone else's master agenda.

"All right," he said. "But Blister and Tempest must meet somewhere to discuss strategy — somewhere where Blister can breathe. If we can find that place, we can kill Tempest."

"Exactly." She regarded him for a long moment, her wings outlined by the sun behind her. "And what's the most important part of our mission?"

"Don't be seen," he said immediately. "Don't get caught. Never let anyone know the NightWings are meddling in the war."

Quickstrike nodded, looking faintly pleased, which was the most pleased she ever managed to look. "Very good. And if you do get caught — "

"I'm a rogue NightWing, exiled from my tribe, causing trouble because I'm insane," Deathbringer said. "Try to get them to kill me quick before they can torture me."

"Especially Blister. I've heard that her torture methods are . . . very effective."

"Don't worry." Deathbringer took to the air and shook the sand off his tail. "You've trained me well."

◆●▶

The Bay of a Thousand Scales was circled by a spur of land that resembled a dragon's tail, getting narrower and narrower as they flew toward the end of it. They searched along the coastline first, looking for any signs of a secret encampment that could hide an entire SandWing army. Quickstrike didn't know exactly how many SandWings had followed Blister out of the desert, but it had to be a substantial number, given how well they were doing in the war.

Usually they searched at night, when their scales were camouflaged by darkness. Deathbringer had found his night vision growing stronger the longer he was away from the Night Kingdom. And they were lucky to have two of the three moons nearly full: Their silver light illuminated any movement on the beaches and cliffs below.

On the second night, they flew over a spot where several fires glowed, and Deathbringer was sure that was it. But when they swooped lower, they found mysteriously small stone buildings, almost like a miniature castle surrounded by little fortresses, and upon further investigation these all turned out to be inhabited by scavengers.

A few of the little two-legged creatures looked up from the battlements as the dragons flew overhead, and one even shot flaming arrows at them, which was pretty adorable.

"I didn't know scavengers could build castles," Deathbringer said to his mother.

"I'm sure they can't," she said. "I'm guessing they found that den the way it was and infested it."

"But who else could have built it?" he asked. "It's too small for dragons."

She shrugged, uninterested, but Deathbringer thought about it for the rest of the night.

Finally they gave up on the coastline and began to search the islands, which was no small task given that there were at least a thousand of them as far as Deathbringer could see.

He offered several ideas on how to lure the dragons out of hiding, but Quickstrike shot them all down.

"Impatience is not a useful quality in an assassin," she said sternly.

"Neither is taking three thousand years to complete a mission," he retorted. They were taking a rest on a small sandbar. Overhead, ominous gray clouds gathered, mumbling about their nefarious plans for the night.

"NightWings play a long game," she informed him. "We use our superior intelligence to tilt events our way, but we must never do it so obviously that the other tribes notice."

"I just want to set *one* palm tree on fire and see who comes to check it out," Deathbringer argued. "They'll never know it was a pair of NightWings."

"No," she said. "Too risky."

"Bah," he said, but didn't press the point. *Obey your elders, do as you're told,* he reminded himself. Even if it meant another long night of flying in what appeared to be an impending hurricane.

The storm caught them suddenly when they were over a stretch of open sea. Rain pelted furiously in their eyes and dragged down their wings as if trying to feed the dragons to the roaring ocean.

"We have to land!" Quickstrike shouted to Deathbringer.

She pointed to the nearest lump of island they could see through the driving rain. But as he turned to follow her, another movement caught his eye, and he batted his mother's tail to make her wait.

Below them, barely staying above the waves, a bedraggled sand-colored dragon was flapping along with his head down. He looked neither left nor right, and he certainly didn't look up to see the NightWings, who exchanged a glance and then followed him.

The SandWing's flight was crooked, but dogged — he was clearly determined to make it through the gale, whatever it took. After a while, Deathbringer saw an island ahead that had to be his destination. It looked wildly overgrown — the kind of place where an army might be hidden below the trees, and two dragons flying overhead could easily miss them.

Deathbringer was fairly unimpressed with the SandWing, who didn't even check once whether he was being followed before he crash-landed on the beach and hurried into the trees.

"That must be it," Quickstrike said. She flicked her forked tongue out and in with a laugh. "We found them."

"Now we wait for Commander Tempest," said Deathbringer.

Quickstrike stretched her wings as lightning flashed around them. "And then we kill her."

Lightning flashed again as she turned, scanning the horizon for an island where they could keep watch and wait out the storm.

"Over there," Deathbringer said, swooping below her.

And then suddenly there was a crash like the sky ripping open. Blinding light sizzled against Deathbringer's eyeballs and Quickstrike let out an agonized shriek. She thudded into him hard and he smelled burning scales.

He scrambled for a hold on her, wet claws slipping on soaked scales. She was too big — he couldn't possibly fly with her, not while she was unconscious, not as far as the next island.

It was all he could do to steer their tumbling course down to the beach where the SandWing had landed. He rolled to land first, cushioning her fall with a jarring shock that vibrated through all his bones.

The torrential downpour continued as they lay there, half buried in wet sand. Deathbringer tried to take a deep breath, but it felt like drowning.

Quickstrike was splayed out in the middle of the beach, her eyes closed and her wings askew like ragged curtains. He couldn't see the spot where the lightning had hit her — it was impossible in the dark against her black scales, with spots still flashing in front of his lightning-dazzled eyes.

But he could see that they were completely exposed here, with Blister camped who knew how many heartbeats away. If she had diligent guards posted, they might have been spotted already. Their only chance was hoping that the hurricane had driven the guards under cover — but even if it had, that wouldn't last.

"Quickstrike," he cried in her ear. He shook her shoulder, but she didn't respond. "Mother, wake up. We have to hide. Mother!"

Nothing. He wiped raindrops from his eyes and scanned the beach. Up by the tree line there was a cluster of fallen palm trees, perhaps hit by lightning in an earlier storm. That would have to work.

Deathbringer tucked his mother's wings in close to her and dug himself into the sand below her, using all his weight to roll her up the beach, one struggling, aching, muscle-screaming step at a time. Wet sand clumped between his claws and splattered into his mouth and coated Quickstrike's scales. He felt as if he was metamorphosing into a MudWing, and maybe from there into some kind of worm, squashed under someone's talon at the bottom of a mud puddle.

But finally, finally he gave one last shove and she slid over the rise and down into a hollow between the fallen trees. With the last bit of his strength, Deathbringer dragged over the biggest palm fronds and rammed one of the trunks into a better position. *Make sure it looks natural. Like it always fell this way.* He scooped sand into an embankment all around his mother until she was as well hidden as he could possibly make her.

His legs were shaking as he returned to the beach with one of the palm fronds. *One more thing to do. Wipe away all our prints, all traces that we were here. Quick, before someone sees.*

The rain might take care of the evidence for him, but his training wouldn't let him risk it. Deathbringer gritted his teeth and swept the beach, trying to hide not only his talon-prints but the churned-up sand trail that led directly to their hiding spot.

The rain was helping, as were the towering waves that were trying to eat the entire beach. Deathbringer tramped around making a mess of the whole area, until at last he felt as though he'd done everything he could. He dragged himself back to his mother, dug himself a hole in the sand, and fell instantly asleep in the howling storm.

◄●►

Two days passed, but Quickstrike didn't wake up. She was breathing, but nothing Deathbringer did could get a response from her. In the daylight he could see an awful burn zigzagged across one of her wings, but all he could do to treat it was keep it cool and wet.

Will she ever fly again?

How am I going to get her home?

And what about the mission?

He knew what Quickstrike would say. The mission comes first. The mission is everything.

If I were the one hit by lightning, she'd have gone ahead and finished the mission already.

That's what she'd want me to do.

That's what she'd order me to do.

If I get it over with, I can focus on how to get her home.

So at midnight on the second day, he left their hiding spot and crept into the island jungle, feeling his way cautiously through the unfamiliar terrain. Strange hoots and yelps came from the trees; he couldn't tell what was bird, monkey, frog, or insect, but they all seemed to have strong opinions about something.

Finally he heard an indisputably dragon sound: talons stamping and voices muttering.

"I hate being on night watch," said one of them. "I swear things are crawling on me."

"Can't see anything anyway with all these toad-spawned trees in the way," grumbled the other.

Deathbringer slipped past them silently. Soon after that he came to a break in the trees and saw a lagoon below him, the still water dappled with silver moonlight. Tents were set up all along the beach. He studied the encampment for a moment, noting that there were no fires and that the tents were all the same color as the sand. From the sky, it would be easy to overlook them.

There also weren't as many tents as he'd expect for a whole army camp. Perhaps the rest of the soldiers were hidden in the trees, or scattered on other islands. *That's what I'd do — spread out over several islands so no one could attack us all at once.*

He crouched lower as three dragons slithered out of the largest tent. In the moonlight, it was hard to be sure, but he thought that two of them had the broad, flat foreheads of MudWings. He could see the dangerous curve of the third dragon's tail; that was definitely a SandWing. Was it Blister herself?

"It's a smart plan," said one of the MudWings. "Did Commander Tempest come up with it?"

"No," said the SandWing coldly.

"Well, we'll need her to make it work. The SeaWings will only risk it if she convinces them to."

"I know." The SandWing lashed her tail. "It would be helpful if they would listen to *me* a little bit more."

"This could put the SandWing stronghold under our control," said the other MudWing. "That could win us the war."

"Yes," hissed the SandWing. "It may have escaped your notice, but that *is* the point of all this."

The second MudWing swung his head toward her with an expression Deathbringer couldn't read in the dark.

"The point for us," he said, "is to keep our tribe safe. You promised Queen Moorhen that an alliance with you would protect us from an invasion by the SeaWings. She only agreed because she knew Commander Tempest could be a serious threat. She does not particularly care who sits on the SandWing throne, and neither do I."

"Commander Tempest will be here tomorrow," the SandWing said smoothly. "We'll reconvene then."

Tomorrow. I could kill her tomorrow and be done with the mission.

Then what? Fly home, report my success, and get help? Could anyone get here in time to save Quickstrike?

Deathbringer wanted to go back and check on Quickstrike, but he thought he shouldn't risk moving around the jungle too much, especially since then he'd have to return during the daytime. So he found a shadowy tree with a good view of the biggest tent and curled onto one of the higher branches to wait.

The next morning was unusually cold, the kind where setting something on fire would have been very helpful. But of course he couldn't do that. Deathbringer rubbed his talons together as quietly as he could. His eyes felt tired, as if someone had rolled heavy boulders up against the back of his eyeballs.

One thing he had noticed since leaving the Night Kingdom was that his sleep patterns seemed to be shifting. In the fortress, he had always lived on a regimented schedule of morning training, but both he and Quickstrike had found themselves staying awake longer and longer each night, and then sleeping later and later each morning. The brighter the moons were, the more wide-awake Deathbringer felt.

He didn't mind the change, although he had to admit it made early-morning assassination watch a lot more painful.

The morning crawled on and the sun scraped slowly up the sky, which remained empty of dragon wings. Nobody arrived. Nobody left. Dragons poked their heads out of their tents or patrolled along the edge of the lagoon. Most of them were SandWings, with a few MudWings here and there. Deathbringer got the feeling that everyone was waiting, exactly as he was.

Finally his attention was caught by an enormous splash off to his right. He lifted his head to look and saw a small whale come surging out of the water, thrashing and twisting. A moment later, sharp blue claws sank into the whale's sides and it was dragged back under, disappearing in a cloud of red bubbles.

He stared at the spot intently and realized that there were ripples extending far out from that spot . . . as if a parade of sea dragons were swimming their way.

Sure enough, a few moments later, an enormous blue-green SeaWing emerged from the water, shaking her wings vigorously. She was powerfully built, as big as Morrowseer, with broad shoulders and gleaming teeth and a healing burn scar on her neck, and she had a trident longer than Deathbringer strapped to her back.

Holy mother of lava, Deathbringer thought. *I'm supposed to kill* THAT?

Commander Tempest was followed by two more SeaWings: a big green male dragon with dark green eyes and gold bands around his ankles, and a wiry female with small eyes and dark gray-blue scales. Behind them, keeping their scales in the water as they eyed the troops on the beach, were about twenty other SeaWing soldiers.

"Blister!" Commander Tempest shouted, stamping one foot in the sand. "We're here! Let's get this over with!"

The SandWing from the night before emerged slowly from her tent, holding her head high. Even from a distance, Deathbringer could see her eyes glittering with danger. A pattern of black diamond scales ran along her back and real black diamonds hung from her ears, outlined in white gold. An aura of menace seemed to surround her.

Even standing next to the towering SeaWing commander, Blister was still the most terrifying dragon on the island.

"So pleased you've finally chosen to join us," Blister said, stopping far enough away that she wouldn't have to look up at Tempest. "Will Queen Coral be attending at last?"

"Ha," Tempest said in a big, jovial voice. "The queen has her own kingdom to run. She won't ever have to meet with you as long as I'm here to handle our strategy summits. But she did send her husband, Gill." The commander swept one wing at the green dragon, nearly knocking him over, but he dodged neatly and gave Blister a charming smile.

"And this is my third-in-command, Piranha," Tempest went on, nodding at the other dragon. "I left my second watching the troops, of course. Make sure they don't have too much fun, ha!" Her booming bark of a laugh was startling every time; a cluster of seagulls nearby kept shooting into the air when it went off, then circling back to land cautiously until it happened again.

"Queen Coral sends her respects," said Gill, bowing, although not very deeply. "She has sent me to open a conversation with you about possible peace negotiations."

"Oh?" Blister glowered at him.

"Yes. We're starting to wonder if this war is really worth it for anyone involved," Gill said. "Perhaps there's a way to reach a diplomatic accord. Maybe by dividing the Kingdom of Sand among the three of you, for instance."

Deathbringer noticed that a number of MudWings had crept closer to listen. Even a few SandWings had stopped what they were doing, their heads tilted toward the cluster of dragons around Blister.

Blister regarded Gill without blinking for a long, tense moment.

"How interesting," she said at last. "I wonder if anyone involved would even consider it. Peace by negotiation. How . . . undragonly."

"I wager I could talk them into it," Gill said, smiling again.

"Would be fine by me," Tempest said. She stamped her foot again, splattering sand on Blister's claws. "I mean, I love being the war commander and all, but it's a messy business, aren't I right? Ha!"

Blister gave her sandy claws a withering look.

Deathbringer had a sudden, worrying thought. *I can't let Gill succeed. Quickstrike said the war must go on — if he talks everyone into peace, the NightWing plan will be ruined.*

But what do I do? Do I have to kill him, too?

That's not in my orders.

And he's married to the queen of the SeaWings. Who knows what new problems I might cause?

So how do I stop him?

His orders weren't sufficient. He had a sudden bracing image of his future — if this was always going to be his job, his orders might *never* be sufficient.

"Well," Blister said, flicking her tongue in and out. "Let's start by reviewing my new attack plan, shall we? I feel confident that if this works, the war will be over without any need for . . . compromises."

"Can't wait to see it," Tempest boomed. She glanced at the biggest MudWing. "Oh, hey, you're here!"

"Yes," Blister said. "We've been waiting for you for a couple of days now." She turned to sweep back into her tent.

"Weapons," the MudWing interjected.

"Right!" Commander Tempest swung the trident off her back and dropped it with a thud on the sand at her feet.

The MudWing stepped forward and placed his spear beside the trident. Blister rolled her eyes, reached into a sheath on her ankle, and tossed a wicked-looking dagger onto the pile of weapons.

Gill, Piranha, two MudWings, and a pair of SandWings did the same with their weapons, and then the entire group vanished into Blister's tent.

Deathbringer studied the discarded objects for a moment: another trident, a twisted white horn that came to a claw-sharp point, a sword, another dagger, and two more spears that matched the MudWing's.

An idea was beginning to form.

→●→

The strategy meeting went on all day, which was plenty of time for Deathbringer to get what he needed from a snoring guard in one of the jungle camps.

He realized that his claws were shaking as he moved into position. He knew he could do what he needed to . . . but he wasn't as certain about escaping afterward.

If I get caught, my life is over. And then what happens to Quickstrike?

He couldn't think about her in this moment. He had to focus on the mission, as she would have ordered.

But is this the right thing to do? Would she approve? Would she tell me to be stealthier?

There was no way to know; he was the only one here who could make this decision.

And they were coming out of the tent now. He had to do this *now*.

Blister emerged first, her face a mask of barely concealed displeasure. Behind her came the MudWing general, and directly behind him was Commander Tempest.

"You're right, you're right," Tempest said, shaking her head. "Between our three armies, this plan could work. I'm real tempted by this idea of a peace accord, though — aren't you, Swamp?"

"General Swamp," corrected the MudWing. "I'd have to ask my queen. We would, above all else, require a promise from the SeaWings to —"

The spear whistled slightly as it flew through the air, giving Commander Tempest just enough time to raise her head and see it coming — but not enough time to get out of the way.

The blade plunged into her heart. Her eyes widened as she stared down at the long wooden shaft piercing her chest.

"Well, son of a starfish," she said, and then toppled over onto the sand like a slow avalanche.

Piranha, just stepping out of the tent, saw her fallen commander and shrieked with rage.

"Tempest!" Gill cried, pushing past Piranha. "Tempest, no! Tempest!" He rolled her onto her back and pressed his claws against the blood spurting from the wound.

It wouldn't help. Deathbringer was too well trained; the spear had landed exactly where he'd aimed and the assassination was complete.

That was only the first part of the plan, though.

"Search the trees!" Piranha roared. "Find who did this!" The SeaWing soldiers leaped from the water and swarmed up the beach.

Deathbringer drew his wings closer and froze, a shadow among shadows in the upper branches of a tree, concealed by several large birds' nests, a wild structure of branches constructed by monkeys, and a giant spiderweb. He could hear dragons thrashing through the bushes below him.

Don't move. Don't move. Don't . . . move . . . a muscle . . .

"There's a note," said one of the SandWings, spotting the leaf that was wedged into the end of the spear. She tugged it loose and spread it on the sand beside Gill, but he was leaning against Tempest's side and his shoulders were shaking with sobs.

Stop feeling guilty, Deathbringer ordered himself. *You're an assassin. This is what you do. You followed orders. It's for a greater cause.*

Would be nice to know what that greater cause is, though.

Blister snatched the note out of her soldier's talons and scanned it rapidly.

THIS IS WHAT WE THINK ABOUT YOUR SECRET DEAL WITH BLISTER. STAY IN THE WATER WHERE YOU BELONG! THE COAST OF THE MUD KINGDOM IS OURS!

For an anxious moment, Deathbringer thought that Blister might set the note on fire, but Piranha seized it first.

"What?" she sputtered, staring at the words on the leaf. She whirled to stare at the weapon. "That's a *MudWing* spear! One of *your* dragons did this!" She stabbed a claw at General Swamp.

"Why would we do that?" he shouted. He grabbed the

note from her and read it. "What secret deal? WHAT SECRET DEAL?"

"There is no secret deal," Blister said. "Someone is trying to break up this alliance, obviously."

Oooooh, Deathbringer thought, impressed with her calm.

"Have you promised the SeaWings part of our land?" General Swamp roared.

"Did you have our commander killed to stop us from getting it?" Piranha snarled back.

"AHA!" he bellowed. "You ADMIT IT!"

"We don't want your stupid land!" Piranha shrieked. "But we're certainly going to take it now!"

Gill looked up, his face streaked with tears. "Wait," he said. "Wait, let's — nobody say anything we might regret — we should —"

"We found these two in the trees up there," called a SeaWing soldier. He and three others pushed two confused MudWings out onto the beach, passing right below Deathbringer's perch. "Exactly where the spear came from."

"We didn't do that!" protested one of the brown dragons. "We don't know anything about it!"

"So someone else snuck past you and did it? And you're the worst guards in the Bay of a Thousand Scales, is that what you're admitting?" Piranha barked.

"Listen, wet nose," the guard snapped back, "you don't know anything about guarding on land, so take your sanctimonious —"

"I demand that these murderers be executed!" Piranha roared.

"Piranha!" Gill tried to protest.

"It wasn't a MudWing!" General Swamp roared back. "It was probably *her*!" He jabbed one claw at Blister. "She never liked Tempest! When you weren't here, she was always complaining about how loud and smelly she was or how everyone always worshipped her like pathetic big-eyed manatees!"

"That's rather inaccurate," Blister protested, raising her voice slightly. "I've never compared anyone to a manatee in my life."

Piranha whirled toward Blister, lashing her tail furiously. "Kill these MudWing assassins right now, or your alliance with the SeaWings is over."

"Touch one scale on their heads and you lose the MudWings forever," hissed General Swamp.

They both glared at Blister. An eerie stillness had fallen over the SandWing; her nostrils flared as if she could smell the treachery in the air.

"SandWings," she said in her cold, hard voice. "Search the island. *Thoroughly.* Turn over every log; climb every tree; wade into every pool. Find the dragon who did this. It will be a SkyWing, or an IceWing, or one of my sisters' SandWings — any SandWing who doesn't belong here. When you find that dragon, bring it to me, and I will kill it, and then we can move on from this foolish distraction."

The SandWing soldiers fanned out immediately, moving with such precision that Deathbringer wondered whether they'd done this kind of search before. He could imagine that Blister was paranoid enough to command something like this regularly.

"And if you find no one?" General Swamp growled.

"Then," Blister said, "it must have been one of your MudWings, don't you agree?"

"I do not," he snapped.

"What are we going to do without her?" Gill said mournfully. He folded Tempest's wings in gently and closed her eyes.

"She's only one dragon," said Blister. "We'll still win the war. Bring me Queen Coral and I'll explain how."

Gill didn't answer. Silence fell over the small group on the beach.

Deathbringer had never been so still for so long. The shadows lengthened, stretching toward night, as SandWings tore through the bushes below him. One even climbed his tree, peering horribly intently at Deathbringer's frozen outline, but when one of her wings got caught in the spiderweb she started cursing and climbed down again.

In the gray twilight, Blister's soldiers began to gather on the edge of the lagoon in front of her, reporting one after another that the island was empty of enemy dragons.

The last pair of soldiers that came in bowed deeply, and then one of them said, "We found someone."

Blister tensed, her tail poised as though she could cut the air around her. "What did you do with them?"

They exchanged a glance. "It's not what you think, Your Majesty," said one. "It can't be the assassin you're looking for. This one's a NightWing, and she's been hit by lightning, and she's unconscious."

"Half dead, I'd say," agreed the other soldier.

Stupid stupid stupid. Deathbringer wanted to rip off his own ears. He should have gone back and hidden her better before carrying out this plan. He should have known Blister would search the island so carefully. *I was so wrapped up in the mission, I completely forgot about protecting Quickstrike.*

"Could someone have been with her?" Blister asked.

"Doubt it," one of the soldiers answered. "Didn't see any other talonprints around her. Looks like she got hit, crashed on the beach, pulled herself to shelter, and lost consciousness. Probably in that storm a couple nights back."

"A NightWing, out here," Blister mused. "How curious. Did you try waking her up?"

"Yeah — yes, Your Majesty — but I doubt she'll ever wake up again. Barely breathing at all, you know?"

"Fine," Blister snapped. "This is clearly irrelevant. Make her completely dead and then come back."

They nodded and flew away.

Deathbringer's life was falling through his talons.

Go after them! his heart screamed. *Stop them! You can kill them easily! Save her!*

But then my cover would be blown. I could never get her out of here without being caught. They'd know I was the one who assassinated Commander Tempest; they'd know I'm not a rogue NightWing acting crazy. They'd kill Quickstrike anyway. They'd kill me, they'd all swear vengeance on the NightWings, and their alliance would be stronger than ever.

All of this would be for nothing.

Silent tears slid down his snout, but he kept his position.

He did not move.

He followed orders.

But this will never happen again, he vowed. *If I ever find someone else to care about, I will not let my mission come first. I will break any order. I'll endanger my own tribe if I have to.*

I will make up for this somehow. Someday.

The good news was, a NightWing messenger was waiting in the agreed-upon spot at the exact agreed-upon time, midnight, one month after Quickstrike and Deathbringer had left the kingdom.

The bad news was, it was Morrowseer.

Well, Deathbringer thought, *here goes nothing.*

"Hello there," he said, landing beside the huge black dragon.

Morrowseer gave him a disdainful look. "You are not worth my breath," he snorted. "Where is Quickstrike?"

"Not coming tonight," Deathbringer said breezily, the way he'd practiced a million times on the way here. "She sent me."

"That's . . ." Morrowseer paused and regarded him for a moment. "Aggravating. I don't do business with sniveling dragonets."

"Then you're in luck," said Deathbringer. "I am firmly anti-sniveling myself."

"I see what she's up to." Morrowseer flicked his tail. "She thought if you both showed up, I might insist on dragging you back home where you belong. But if it's just you, I have to let you go so you can take the new instructions back to her. Very clever."

Deathbringer kept his face neutral. "I've always admired Quickstrike's intelligence, too."

"That was quite a stunt you pulled with Slaughter," Morrowseer said with an affected yawn. "You're probably better off staying out of the kingdom until Vengeance cools down. I wouldn't hold your breath, though, since to my knowledge he was named quite appropriately."

"I'm not going to spend a moment worrying about Vengeance," Deathbringer said. "I'm here to report. Commander Tempest is dead. Blister's alliance with the SeaWings and MudWings has been destabilized. Our prediction is that the MudWings are going to abandon her altogether."

"Really?" It was pretty satisfying to see Morrowseer so surprised. "That's — better news than we had hoped for. That should slow her down significantly. She won't get far with only SeaWings."

"A potential area of concern is whether the MudWings will align themselves with one of the other sisters," Deathbringer went on. "And we recommend keeping a close eye on a SeaWing named Gill, who appears to be intent on brokering peace.

"Although," Deathbringer added quickly, seeing the glint in the other dragon's eyes, "we wouldn't recommend another SeaWing assassination this soon after the first one. Could be suspicious, destabilize things *too* much, shift the power too far out of Blister's talons."

"True," said Morrowseer. "We'll keep an eye on the situation. In the meanwhile, you have a new assignment."

"Already? I mean — good. Who is the target?"

"A SandWing general under Burn." Morrowseer handed Deathbringer a scroll. "All the information is in there. You should be able to find him in the Kingdom of Sand. Another one who's a bit too smart and too effective for our liking."

Deathbringer unrolled the scroll, breathing a small plume of fire so he could see the rough sketch and the name written underneath.

"General Six-Claws."

"Shouldn't be too hard to identify," Morrowseer said dryly. "Presumably he'll be the one with six claws."

Deathbringer rolled up the scroll. "And meet back here in a month?" he asked.

"I'm giving you three months for this one. The Kingdom of Sand is bigger than you think, with fewer places for black dragons to hide. Your mother will have to teach you a lot of new skills for this mission."

A stab of sorrow, another in a thousand moments of hidden grief.

"I'm sure she will," said Deathbringer. "See you in three months."

Morrowseer lifted off first, winging north without a backward glance. Deathbringer watched his serpentine shape outlined against the moons until it was out of sight, and then he unrolled the scroll again.

Maybe General Six-Claws didn't have to die, exactly.

Maybe he just needed a good reason to stop working for Burn.

After all, if Deathbringer could break the MudWing alliance with Blister, maybe he could shift some other game pieces around as well.

Maybe there were other ways to be a great assassin, if you could see the bigger picture.

I'll make Morrowseer tell me everything one day.

For now . . . let's see how creative I can get with these orders.

WINGS OF FIRE

OF

FIRE

WINGLETS #3: DESERTER

Note: This story begins before the
War of SandWing Succession and ends shortly
after the events of Winglets #2: *Assassin*.

Unlike most dragons, Six-Claws had a remarkably happy childhood.

His mother was one of Queen Oasis's most trusted guards and his father was the head chef in the queen's kitchen. Ostrich and Quicksand's lives were devoted to the queen, but Six-Claws and his two sisters came a close second. The family was almost always together.

His mother taught him how to keep watch and how to fight and how to defend his queen at all costs. His father taught him how to make camel shish kebab and date soufflé. His sisters, meanwhile, taught him that you should really not tell your sisters who you have a crush on, unless you want the entire palace to know about it.

Six-Claws loved growing up in the SandWing palace, surrounded by open sky and rolling desert dunes as far as the eye could see in every direction. He learned to fly earlier than any of the other dragonets who hatched in his year. He signed up for every patrol, whether it was harvesting

brightsting cacti or hunting desert foxes or firebombing suspected dragonbite viper lairs. He liked to be useful. He liked
to be *doing* things.

And of course, since his parents were loyal to Queen
Oasis, he was loyal to her as well. If anyone asked, he
could have rattled off a list of reasons why she was a great
queen. This was a conversation he heard regularly around
the dinner table in the small barracks room assigned to his
family.

It wasn't until he was five years old that he learned there
might one day be a different SandWing queen.

That is, he knew intellectually, from school lessons, that a
queen's daughter, granddaughter, sister, or niece could challenge her to a fight to the death, and whoever won would
be queen. But he'd never imagined anyone doing that to *his*
queen.

He was in the kitchens that afternoon, pounding beetles
into a glittering black powder for his father, when his mother
came in. She nudged Six-Claws affectionately with her wing
as she passed him. His father looked up from one of the caul-
drons, steam obscuring his face.

"Did you hear?" Ostrich asked him. "Another princess
hatched today. The queen is calling her Blaze."

"Really?" Quicksand dragged a tray of bread loaves out of
the oven. "She's keeping it, then?"

"Her Majesty has always said she'd allow three heirs, no
more," said Ostrich, taking the other edge to help him lift it

onto the stone table. "So if she keeps Blaze, one of the others has to go."

Quicksand snorted. "That's easy. The one who likes cutting the legs off jackrabbits just to see what they'll do." He wrinkled his snout. "There was one flopping around the courtyard shrieking for an hour yesterday. Do you know how hard it is to stuff olives under those conditions?"

"She's creepy," Ostrich agreed, "but the one Queen Oasis *should* get rid of is the other daughter, Blister. That dragon always looks like she's murdering you with her eyes. But it won't be either of them. It'll be the queen's sister, you'll see. She's much closer to challenging Her Majesty than the daughters are. It makes sense to dispose of her."

"Challenge the queen?" Six-Claws interrupted, startled out of eavesdropping. "Why would anyone do that?"

"To become the next queen," Quicksand answered with an amused expression. "Because she thinks she'd be better at it than the current queen."

"No one could be a better queen than Queen Oasis!" Six-Claws insisted forcefully.

"That's absolutely right, dear," his mother said, wrapping one wing around him. "Don't worry, I'm sure she'll be queen for a long while yet. Although whoever comes after her, we'll be loyal to her, too."

Ostrich was right about one thing: by the next day, the queen's one remaining sister had vanished into thin air, and nobody ever mentioned her name again.

After that, Six-Claws watched the SandWing princesses differently. Now they weren't just royalty. They were deadly. They were a threat to his queen.

Well . . . two of them were.

The youngest daughter, Blaze, turned out to be one of the silliest dragonets Six-Claws had ever met. As soon as she could walk she started following any dragon she could find who was wearing treasure. The more sparkles, the better; she had a knack for zeroing in on the dragons with the most glittering jewelry.

Six-Claws suspected that if she ever killed her mother, it wouldn't be for power or a throne; it would be for a pair of diamond earrings. And she wouldn't do it with her claws or her fire — she'd do it by annoying the queen to death.

He watched the princesses for two years, but his first interaction with them didn't come until he was seven years old . . .

◄●►

"My sisters are up to something."

Six-Claws looked up, squinting at the figure silhouetted against the blinding sun. He'd been trying to dig out a stubborn ball of roots from the palace garden for the better part of the morning. His muscles ached and his scales were hot enough to fry snake eggs on.

"Sisters are always up to something," he said, resting his arms on his shovel.

"True. But whatever *my* sisters are planning could bring down the kingdom." The other dragon turned his head into the light, and Six-Claws tensed, recognizing Prince Smolder. The prince was from the same hatching as Princess Blister, so he was two years older than Six-Claws. They'd been on several missions together, although they'd rarely spoken to each other.

And he was right. *His* sisters were not ordinary dragons.

"Which sisters?" Six-Claws asked. "How do you know?"

"Burn and Blister," said the prince. "They've been whispering together all morning."

That was definitely a bad sign. The two older princesses generally avoided each other as much as possible. If they were conspiring, that could only mean bad things for someone.

"Why are you telling me?" Six-Claws asked cautiously.

"Well," Smolder said, "I'm not sure what else to do. You seem kind of strong and sensible. I was hoping you could come up with something." He flicked his venomous tail around and sat down with an expectant expression.

"You should ask them what they're up to," Six-Claws suggested, jabbing at the root ball again. "You're their brother. They might tell you."

"Ha ha!" The prince gave an odd shudder. "And draw their attention to me instead? No, thank you, that's not how survival works in this family."

Six-Claws considered for a moment what it must be like to live in a family where "survival" was an issue of sibling dynamics. "They can't be going after the queen," he mused. "Not together. But I could warn my mother, just in case."

"Who else would they be plotting against?" Smolder wondered.

Realization hit Six-Claws like a lightning bolt. "Your little sister," he said. He dropped the shovel and his wings snapped open. "Knock the number of heirs down to two." He scrambled out of the hole, shaking dirt off his claws. "Where is Blaze?"

"How would I know?" Prince Smolder jumped out of the way of the cascades of dust coming off Six-Claws. "So you'll take care of it?"

"Aren't you going to help me?" Six-Claws frowned at the prince. "Don't you want to protect your little sister?"

"I am!" Smolder shifted warily on his talons. "By telling you, and then staying alive so I can do it again next time! I'm sure you can handle it." He took another step back, then turned and hurried off into the palace.

"Wait!" Six-Claws called. "What about your brothers? Where are they?"

"Out on patrol," Smolder yelled back before he whisked around a corner and vanished.

Six-Claws heaved a frustrated sigh. He didn't have time to run after a cowardly prince. Apparently he had to find the youngest princess before something terrible happened to her. Which did not sound like his job at all, but unlike

Smolder, he wasn't the kind of dragon to pass it off to someone else.

The wingery was close by; he could check there first. Most dragonets in the palace played in the shelter of its walls until they were two years old, under the watchful eye of a pair of ancient SandWings. Six-Claws remembered their creaky voices telling stories about how they'd taught young Oasis to fly when she was just a tiny mite herself. The wingery was open to anyone who lived in the palace, so the children of servants and nobles all grew up together — princesses and future pot-scrubbers side by side.

With no time to waste, he hopped onto the wall of the garden and flew there instead of taking the cooler indoor passageways.

The courtyard for the dragonets featured a sunken pool in the middle, where they could splash and cool off in the midday heat. This was overlooked by a shaded pavilion with long white curtains on the three open sides. Six-Claws had spent two painful years in that pavilion, struggling to learn to read and to count little piles of red pebbles. Sitting still for that long was the worst. That was not his idea of doing something; that was just torture.

The rest of the courtyard was set up to help the dragonets learn to fly: ledges at different heights, soft piles of sand to land in, claw holds and perches everywhere. And of course, in one corner, a first aid station stocked with lots of brightsting cactus, which was the only antidote to the venom in a SandWing's tail. The venom didn't come in until a dragonet was closer to three years old — luckily for everyone — but at this age they had a tendency to crash into everything or leap onto their parents without looking first, so there was a lot of bandaging and antidote-administering required. The young dragons also spent a *lot* of time practicing how to be aware of their tails and everyone else's, so they could eventually be safely released into the rest of the palace.

Six-Claws flew down into the courtyard, scanning the pool and the flying stations. No sign of Blaze. She had just turned two, so she might consider herself too old for the wingery now, but he couldn't think where she might go next. He stuck his head between the curtains of the pavilion and an entire class of SandWing dragonets twisted around to stare at him.

"Yes?" snapped the wizened old dragon at the front.

"Is Princess Blaze here?" Six-Claws asked.

The teacher snorted. "Do you see anyone drawing tiaras in the margins of their history scrolls? Then, no."

"Do you know where she might be?"

"My guess? Drooling over a pile of gems or sharing adoring sighs with a mirror somewhere," he snapped. "Stop interrupting our lesson."

"I can help you look," offered the dragon beside the teacher, and Six-Claws noticed him for the first time. He was older than the other dragonets, probably about four years old, with powerful sandy-yellow wings and flashing black eyes.

"Your mother said to stay here and learn the job," the teacher growled.

"Oh, but this sounds *very* important," the other dragon answered, practically leaping over the little dragonets between him and Six-Claws. "I'm sure I'll be back soon!" He seized Six-Claws by the arm and muttered, "Let's go, quick."

Six-Claws backed out of the pavilion and jumped to the nearest balcony. The young dragon followed him, ignoring the wheezing shouts of the teacher, and then they both soared up to one of the higher palace towers. The wind tugged at their wings with unusual strength, and when Six-Claws glanced up, he realized the sky was darker than it should be for midday in the desert.

"Thank you for getting me out of there," the dragon panted as they landed. "I'm Dune."

"Six-Claws. What was that all about?"

Dune immediately looked at Six-Claws's talons — yes, he had six claws on each of his front feet instead of the usual five; thanks so much for letting everyone know right away, parents — and then tried very hard to pretend that he hadn't. "I'm supposed to be in training to become a teacher. My parents are both teachers, and they think working in the wingery forever would be just the perfect job for me." He wrinkled his snout.

"You sound thrilled about that idea," Six-Claws said. He was only half listening; his attention was on the palace compound spread out below him as he searched for any sign of the littlest princess. Far off on the western horizon, a wall of ominous clouds was gathering.

"I guess minding dragonets runs in the family," Dune said. He shuddered. "But I hope I don't have to do it for the rest of my life. Dragonets are so aggravating. I want to be a soldier! I want to fight in battles and do glorious things and be a hero!" He flared his wings enthusiastically. "What do you want to do?"

"Whatever my queen needs me to do," Six-Claws answered, with complete honesty. He wanted to serve his tribe and be the most useful dragon he could possibly be. "Now think. Where could Blaze be?"

"The royal treasury," Dune said promptly. "Hoping her mother will come by to unlock it so she can roll in the jewels. That dragonet is as bad as a scavenger. I'm not sure she thinks about anything except treasure, and she doesn't even care about which items are worth more than others. We tried to turn her obsession into a math lesson, but she prefers the prettiest ones, even if they're fake."

"Go check the treasury," Six-Claws said. He turned toward the other side of the tower, intending to search the other pools — but then something caught his attention.

A flash of light out in the desert.

A tremor of movement across the sand.

A small dragonet, trekking out toward the incoming storm.

"What is she *doing*?" he yelped. He couldn't tell for sure that it was Blaze, but whoever it was needed to get back to the palace right away.

"Whoa," Dune said, squinting beside him. "Is that the princess? Why would she be out in the dunes by herself? By all the lizards, she is going to get *crushed* by that sandstorm."

"Get help," Six-Claws said. He shoved Dune back and spread his wings. "Tell the queen, if you can."

"You're going to *get* her?" Dune said. "Why? You'll *both* get crushed."

"Because you never leave dragonets in danger," Six-Claws answered, startled that anyone would need to have that explained to him.

"You don't? Even if it means risking your own — all right, all right," Dune said, cutting himself off at the look on Six-Claws's face. "No dragonets in danger, got it."

Six-Claws threw himself off the tower and soared over the palace and out into the desert, beating his wings as fast as he could.

He was lucky to be strong and fast. By the time he caught up to Princess Blaze, the wind was whipping furiously around them, flinging harsh particles of sand into their eyes.

But she was still struggling onward, walking instead of flying, her wings tucked in and her head bent and her eyes closed.

Six-Claws landed in front of her and spread his wings, shielding her from the storm for a moment. She rubbed her face and looked up at him, blinking in surprise.

"Where are you going?" he asked.

"To get my favorite crown," she said spiritedly. "Don't you try to stop me, you big-shouldered bighead!"

He tilted his head. "What crown?"

"The one Agave stole and hid out here, according to Camel, who heard it from Parch, who is her best friend, so it's completely true, and I'm going to get it back, because it's MINE and Mommy gave it to me." Blaze suddenly sat down and lifted her chin. "Unless you go get it for me. Ooo, *that* sounds like a good idea."

"We can't," he said. "This storm is too dangerous." *And I'm guessing that whole story is a lie planted somewhere along the way by Burn and Blister,* he thought. "You must get back to the palace."

"NO!" Blaze shouted. "I *want* what's *mine*." She tried to stomp past him, but the wind immediately seized her wings and flung her backward onto the sand.

"Ow!" she cried, trying to sit up. "That hurt! Something hurt me!"

Six-Claws looked over his shoulder. An enormous wall of dust clouds was bearing down on them, reaching from the sand all the way up to the sky and moving fast. There was no more time to treat the princess like precious royalty.

"We have to go!" he shouted. He threw his arms around her, pinning her wings to her sides, and lunged into the air.

"My croooooooooowwwwwn!" she wailed. She plunked her head on his shoulder and cried all the way back to the palace.

The princess was heavier than she looked, but the wind was with them now, hurtling them in front of the storm. As they got closer, Six-Claws could see doors and windows slamming closed all over the palace. The dragons were preparing for the onslaught of sand.

Wait, he thought desperately. *Wait for us. We're coming.*

And then finally, as his strength began to give out and he felt the cloud right on his tail, he saw a shutter open in one of the walls. Dune leaned out, waving a huge white cloth to get his attention.

Six-Claws put on one last burst of speed and threw himself through the open window, tucking himself to crash-land on the floor with Blaze on top of him. They skidded part of the way across the room, and he could hear the cries of dragons leaping out of their way.

"Did you bring the *entire* desert in with you?" one of them yelped.

"Idiots! Waiting till the last minute!"

"Don't you know anything about sandstorms?"

"We should have left you out there!"

"Hey, that's Princess Blaze," said someone else, and a kind of hush fell over the room.

Six-Claws blinked, feeling sand cascading from the corners of his eyes. His vision was still blurred, but he could see that they were in one of the great halls where Oasis hosted feasts and dances. Normally sunlight filled the hall, but it was dark with all the shutters and doors closed, and only a few torches had been lit so far. Circles of warm firelight reflected off the scales and dark eyes of the dragons gathered around them.

He let go of the princess and sat up, trying to catch some of the sand that slid off his wings before it made even more of a mess on the floor.

"RrrrrrROAR!" Blaze shouted, shoving him away. She jumped to her feet and shook herself vigorously, covering him and the room and the dragons around them with even more sand. "You ruined everything and now I'll never find it! MOOOMMY!!!"

"Your mother is overseeing the sandstorm lockdown," said a tall, burly dragon, shoving through the crowd to stand over her. "So you can tell *me* what exactly you were doing so far outside the palace."

Blaze puffed up her chest. "You're not the boss of me!"

"I'm one of them," he said sternly. "I *am* your father."

Six-Claws tried to rub away the grit in his eyes so he could see better. Char was the queen's husband, referred to by most SandWings as the king, although he had only as much power as Queen Oasis let him have. Sometimes he went everywhere with the queen, welcomed into advisory meetings and diplomatic gatherings, and then sometimes they would fight and he'd be exiled from the palace for months at a time.

According to Six-Claws's parents, it was safest to be polite and respectful to Char, but never get too close, because you wouldn't want the queen to associate you with him the next time Char fell out of favor.

As Blaze launched into a long, complicated story about her friends and her stolen crown, Six-Claws turned and found Dune behind him, wide-eyed.

"That was alarming," Dune said. "I thought you weren't going to make it back."

Six-Claws shrugged. "We did. I'd better go shake off this sand in one of the baths."

"Father," said a cold voice, slicing through Blaze's breathless narrative. "Shouldn't we ask the name of the dragon who took our little sister out into such terrible danger?"

A chill like midnight in the desert slithered down Six-Claws's spine. He watched the crowd part around Princess Blister as she stepped forward. Her obsidian-black eyes raked over Six-Claws. He could practically see her mind analyzing him and fitting him into a category — something like *Irksome Nuisance* or *Idiot Who Ruined My Plan*.

"He didn't take her out there!" Dune said, raising his tail defensively. "He *saw* her out there alone and *rescued* her, that's what he did!"

"Ah," said Blister. Her tail rattled softly on the floor. "Really. What a hero."

"Right," said Dune, subsiding. "That's what he is. His name is Six-Claws. And I'm Dune, by the way."

"SIX-Claws?" Blaze interrupted. She wriggled out of her father's arms and flounced over to inspect Six-Claws's talons. "Ew! Three moons! You really do have six claws on each foot! That's so weird! I can't believe you touched me with those!" She leaned closer to stare at the extra claws, then jumped back quickly when he pulled his talons into his chest.

Six-Claws felt as if his face was burning. No one had made fun of his odd talons in years, not since his first month in the wingery. He'd always worked hard to prove that it made no difference — he was as valuable as any other dragon. It didn't change anything about what he could do. It just . . . looked odd.

"Yeeeeeeee," Blaze said scornfully. She held out her own perfect, beautiful talons, decorated with three glittering rings. "I'm so glad *I* have the right number of claws."

Right then, deep in his heart, Six-Claws decided that he sincerely hoped Blaze would *never* be queen of the SandWings.

"I'm sure what my daughter is trying to say," Char interjected, "is thank you for saving her life." He gently steered Blaze away from Six-Claws, toward the mirrors across the hall. The little SandWing took one look at herself, gasped in horror, and stormed off toward the baths, radiating outrage.

"We should reward such a brave hero," Blister purred, slithering an inch closer to Six-Claws. "I can think of a few missions he'd be *perfect* for . . ."

A few missions I'm not likely to come back from, Six-Claws thought with a shiver.

"I have a better idea," Char said, cutting her off. Blister narrowed her eyes at him, but he didn't seem to notice. "Brave and strong and a swift flier for your age — how would you like to join the army, Six-Claws? We could use a soldier like you. You could make your way up to captain pretty fast, maybe general one day."

"If that's what the queen wants, sir," Six-Claws said. It was probably safer than whatever Blister had in mind for him. His mother would approve. And soldiers were useful, weren't they? Even in times of peace, like now, there were always skirmishes going on with the SkyWings or IceWings.

"I'll see to it," Char said with a nod.

Something jabbed Six-Claws in the side and he whipped around, tail up, before realizing it was Dune, with a very meaningful expression on his face.

"Uh," Six-Claws said. "My, um . . . my friend Dune helped, too."

"Oh, yes?" said Char. "Would you like to join the army as well, dragonet?"

"Yes, please, sir!" Dune said eagerly.

"Hmmm. You're a bit young, but we can put you in basic training for now. I'll have you two assigned to the same battalion." Char nodded again, looking pleased with himself, and wandered away.

Outside, the wind was howling and rattling the shutters with enormous fury. Six-Claws had a feeling he'd be sweeping sand out of every crevice in the palace tomorrow.

Except he wouldn't be, if Char did as he'd promised. He'd be in soldier training instead, set on a path to a new future. With a new best friend, apparently; Dune was beaming from ear to ear, as though Six-Claws had saved *him* instead of Blaze.

He felt eyes watching him, and when he turned, he saw Blister fix a malevolent glare on him before she slipped out of the room.

I mustn't forget I have a new enemy now, too.

And a new reason to hope that Queen Oasis lives for a very, very long time.

The night Queen Oasis died, Six-Claws and Dune were off duty. That is, they were not scheduled for any soldiers' duties, but they were on duty in a different way: watching over a weeping prince to make sure he didn't do anything regrettable.

"She's gone," Smolder sobbed, plunking his head on his arms and flopping his wings over the table. Several glasses of cactus cider went crashing to the floor and shattered around their talons. "I'm never going to see her again."

Smolder's two brothers exchanged an exasperated glance over his head.

"That's your own fault," said Singe. He nudged a shard of glass away from his feet and beckoned for Dune to sweep it up. "If you hadn't made it so serious, Mother wouldn't have had to intervene."

"You *know* how she feels about any of us getting married," Scald agreed. "You've always known it."

"Yeah, it's a simple policy," said Singe. "No marriage, no dragonets, no extra heirs causing problems. As long as we follow the queen's rules, she leaves us alone."

"Couldn't you keep it casual like the rest of us?" Scald added. "I have three girlfriends right now and everyone's perfectly happy and *not* serious. And *safe*." He lifted his claws as Dune swept around them. Six-Claws slid another pitcher of cider onto the table.

"But Palm was different," Smolder cried. "I loved her. We would have gone away forever and never come back! Mother didn't ever have to see us again!" He lifted his head and turned teary, pleading eyes to Six-Claws. "Have you heard anything? Do you know where she is?"

"No," Six-Claws admitted uncomfortably. "I'm sorry." He was glad he didn't know. He felt very grateful that he hadn't been one of the soldiers sent to deal with Smolder's true love.

"Smolder, come on," Singe said, sitting down beside him and putting one wing over his younger brother's back. "You're not an idiot. You know perfectly well she's dead."

"She *isn't*," Smolder yelled, flinging him off. "She can't be! Mother is cruel but she wouldn't do *that*."

"Of course she would," Scald said. "Do you really not remember our aunts? And how they vanished in this exact same way?"

Six-Claws retreated to the far wall, where he could stare out the window. He didn't like to be reminded of the terrible things Queen Oasis had done to hang on to her throne — and whatever she'd done to Palm hit a little too close to home. He *knew* Palm. She'd worked in the kitchens with his father for a little while, back before both his father and Char had died from the weird sickness that swept the palace a few years ago.

Palm was a sweet, clever, nervous dragon who adored Smolder and was terrified of the queen. She would never have raised dragonets to challenge Oasis. He was sure she would have happily disappeared into the desert with Smolder and never bothered the queen again.

But they'd been caught while they were trying to elope, and now Palm had really disappeared, most likely never to bother anyone ever again.

He sighed, staring out at the three crescent moons that carved up the sky. A shadow flashed overhead, huge and moving fast. Was that . . . the queen? Flying out of the palace at this hour of the night?

That was strange.

"Why doesn't she just *kill me, too*?" Smolder wailed. There was another thump, and another crash of glass splintering.

Dune sidled up beside Six-Claws. "Hey. Did you hear what General Needle said about me today?"

"Something admiring, I assume." Six-Claws smiled at his friend. After all these years, they were still paired together by everyone, for everything. Six-Claws had risen to colonel in the SandWing army, and Dune was always a few steps behind him — a captain at the moment, but sure to become a major any day.

"She said I have more promise than any officer she's ever seen." Dune lifted his chin, glowing with pride. "She said I have extraordinarily strong wings for a SandWing — almost like a SkyWing's! She said I'd be commanding armies of my own in no time."

"She's right," Six-Claws agreed. "Do you smell something weird?"

"No," said Dune, sounding ruffled. "Can we get back to talking about how amazing I am, please?"

Six-Claws stuck his nose out the window, sniffing. "It smells like . . . mammal. But not one of the usual desert animals."

Suddenly a fierce roar tore through the night. A blast of fire lit up the sky beyond the palace wall, followed by more roaring, wild and agonized as though someone was being murdered.

"What is *that*?" Dune cried.

In the room behind them, all three princes were on their feet, blinking and startled.

"It sounded like Mother," said Scald. "But I thought she was asleep."

"Let's go find out." Six-Claws darted out of the room with the others behind him. They raced to the nearest courtyard, opened their wings, and flowed over the palace rooftops. The roaring had stopped, leaving only echoes like shredded holes in the air.

Other dragons joined them, calling to one another in confusion, and so it was a fair crowd that came over the top of the outer walls together . . .

. . . and found the queen lying dead in the sand.

Somebody shrieked, a long wordless cry of rage. It might have been Scald, or it might have been Six-Claws's mother, Ostrich, now pushing past everyone to crouch beside the body. It might have been both of them, or himself, or everyone together.

"Who did this?" Ostrich yelled. "Who killed our queen?"

"Was there a duel?" another dragon asked. "Did I miss it?"

"I didn't hear about a challenge," Singe answered, looking around blankly. "In the middle of the night? Out here? With no witnesses?"

Burn suddenly landed with a violent *thump* on the sand, knocking two dragons over. She stormed forward and glared down at the queen's corpse, quivering with rage.

Ostrich swallowed and took a step back, dipping her head to signal cautious respect.

Burn just stood there, breathing heavily.

After a moment, Ostrich ventured, "Was it you, Your Highness? Are you now our queen?"

Burn growled, low and deep in her throat. "No," she snarled. "I didn't kill her." Ostrich started to raise her head and Burn snapped, "But it wasn't Blister either! I just saw her!"

"Was it . . . Blaze, then?" someone in the crowd asked.

There was an awkward pause as everyone tried to imagine the queen's spacey daughter successfully attacking her. Six-Claws looked around and realized Blaze wasn't even there. *She probably slept right through all this noise. Wearing jeweled earplugs or buried in expensive pillows.*

"It wasn't any of us," Blister's voice said icily from a shadow near the palace wall. She stalked across the sand, flicking her tail menacingly. "Mother wasn't killed by *any* of her daughters."

She faced Burn across the queen's body, each of them sizzling with coiled tension. Burn was older and bigger than Blister, with more battle experience and the scars to show for it. But Six-Claws knew that Blister was smarter . . . and that made him truly unsure who would win in a fight.

"So . . ." Singe asked carefully. "If none of you killed her . . . then, um . . . who's our next queen?"

Blister hissed, dragging one claw through the sand. "I was going to challenge her soon," she said.

"So was I," Burn snapped back.

Six-Claws wondered if that was true for either of them. As scary as they were, he couldn't imagine either of them defeating Queen Oasis.

But clearly *someone* had. Why would anyone murder the queen, unless it was to get her throne?

Revenge, his mind whispered. Beyond his sisters, lit by the pale moonlight, Smolder's eyes were shining. He was nothing but happy to see his mother dead.

But Six-Claws had been with Smolder when they'd heard the roars. Even if Smolder had wanted to kill his mother for what happened to Palm, he couldn't have done it tonight.

"Maybe you two should fight right now," Scald suggested to his sisters. "Whoever wins gets to be queen. That seems fair, right?"

Blister shot him an unreadable but unpleasant look.

"Not exactly fair to Blaze, though," Singe pointed out, and got his own withering glare from both sisters. "Yeah, all right, I know. You two duke it out."

The idea made sense to Six-Claws. A simple fight to the death, the way it had always been, with an obvious winner. The SandWings needed a queen. They should get it over with.

Years later, Six-Claws would often try to imagine how history might have turned out if the sisters had fought that night. He could never decide if it would have been better — no twenty-year war — or worse — one of these two as queen of the SandWings, unchallenged and unstoppable.

Burn curled her talons, ready to lunge at her sister.

"This hardly seems like the time or place," Blister said calmly, taking a slight step away from Burn. "I mean, priorities, my dear brothers. Surely first we *must* find out who did this to our poor beloved mother." She tilted her head at Burn and whispered, "Besides, we don't have the Eye of Onyx."

Not many dragons heard her, but Six-Claws was close enough to catch her words. He didn't understand them, though. There was an Eye of Onyx in the treasury, but what did that have to do with dueling for the throne?

"Right," Burn said, slowly opening her claws again. "Of course. Who killed our mother. That's what we need to figure out," she said, raising her voice to address all the gathered dragons. "Admit it now, whoever did this! Don't make us start gouging out your eyes!"

A shuffling flutter ran through the crowd as everyone stared at everyone else, searching for a guilty expression or bloody talons.

Bloody talons, Six-Claws thought. *How did the queen die?* He looked down at the sand around the body, searching for clues. He noticed that the odd mammal smell was stronger out here. And then he saw for the first time that there was a small spear sticking out of the queen's eye.

He crouched, peering closer. It wasn't a dragon-sized spear; it was only about as long as his foreleg and so thin he could probably snap it between his teeth. Was this what had killed her? This tiny thing?

He scanned the rest of her body for other wounds and discovered the strangest thing of all.

Someone had cut off her venomous tail barb.

"Three moons," he said. "Who would —"

"Search the area," Burn commanded. She seemed to be swelling to twice her normal size, her wings flaring and her voice suddenly ringing like a queen's. "Whoever did this can't have gotten far. We will find them and punish them!"

The SandWings immediately spread out and started shooting flames into all the shadows or poking the dunes with their tails. Their shouts and growls filled the night, and Six-Claws thought he would not want to be the murderer, hiding somewhere nearby. Even anything that wasn't the murderer, like a desert rat, was liable to get stomped by a crusading dragon tonight.

He stared at the small spear again.

Everything started to click into place in his brain.

That scent . . .

The spear was too small for dragons . . . but there was one other animal that was rumored to use spears.

An animal notorious for trying to steal treasure from dragons, no matter how often they got eaten in the process.

"Hey!" Smolder shouted, digging in a sand dune several feet away. "I found something!"

Burn's head snapped up. "What is it?" she barked.

"It's —" Smolder stopped and looked up, confusion written all over his face. "It's a scavenger."

The next few years passed in an exhausting blur. Six-Claws was one of the dragons who chased down the scavengers that had escaped with the queen's tail barb and the stolen treasure; he was there when Burn set their dens on fire and burned all the scavengers' homes to the ground. He helped to hunt through the ashes and then, when they found no treasure, flew back to the palace behind Burn, only to discover that the SandWing treasury had been completely emptied. Four rooms full of gems and gold — all of it gone, vanished into thin air, presumably stolen by the scavengers, although no one could figure out how or where they'd put it.

He was there for the councils and arguments and trials that followed, everyone fighting over who should be the next queen and how it should be decided. He was in the palace the night that Blister took off with half the army, and he was there the night Blaze escaped and fled north with a squadron of loyal guards. In fact, both times he was approached by friends and fellow soldiers, asking him to join them in supporting the dragon they wanted to be queen.

But he said no. His mother had decided to be loyal to Burn, so he was going to do the same thing. He didn't like Burn . . . but he liked her sisters much less. Burn, at least, would be a strong queen, unlike Blaze, and a queen with no secret malevolent plans, which was more than he could say for Blister.

It turned out, though, that there was one thing Burn loved more than mutilating animals, and that was war. When she heard that Blister was negotiating alliances with the SeaWings and MudWings, intending to bring their armies with her to fight for the SandWing throne, Burn was horribly delighted. As she said to General Needle, in Six-Claws's presence, two sisters out there lurking and scheming was just annoying — but armies coming to attack her, *that* she could handle. *That* meant violence and mayhem and fun.

She sent Prince Smolder to the Sky Kingdom immediately to forge an alliance with their queen, Scarlet. She also tried to contact the IceWings, which was how she discovered that they were protecting Blaze and considering joining the new war themselves.

"I hope they do!" Burn cried gleefully, storming through the construction going on outside the palace. Queen Oasis had been buried where she fell, and a monument was raised over her grave. Burn had ordered another layer of thick walls built all around the outside, beyond the monument, turning the palace into an unassailable stronghold. "More dragons to fight! More territory to conquer! We'll crush them all in a matter of weeks!"

It wasn't a matter of weeks. The war dragged on, and on, and on for years, and in that time Six-Claws saw his mother and way too many of his friends die in battle, and he fought way too many faces he had once considered brothers-in-arms.

But he kept fighting. He did as he was ordered. He was promoted, and then promoted again, until he became General Six-Claws. He stayed loyal to Queen Burn, because loyalty ran deep in his blood . . . and because he didn't see any other choice.

It was getting harder, though. When Burn had her brother Singe killed for, as far as Six-Claws could tell, "annoying her," he felt his soul sinking further into despair.

What kind of dragon was he following?

He couldn't imagine describing her good qualities, the way he had once been able to list all the things that were great about Queen Oasis. He was having a hard time coming up with even one, these days.

One night about two weeks after Singe's death, Six-Claws flew back to camp with his battalion after a particularly crushing battle with the IceWings in which he'd lost four good dragons.

And more than that, perhaps even worse: Dune had been badly injured. Dune, the one dragon who had stayed by his side and survived all these years. One of his forearms had been bitten nearly in two and his wing had been hit by a blast of frostbreath. Six-Claws hoped there was still time to reverse the damage and heal his friend. He helped carry Dune all the way back from the battle site.

They'd set up their small city of tents not far from where the desert shifted into rocky hills, then tundra and the Ice Kingdom. Technically the rocky terrain was part of the

Kingdom of Sand, so he could have made camp even closer to the IceWing border. But his dragons needed to sleep on sand and return to the desert at night for their morale. If he'd forced them farther north, they might have had shorter flights to their battles, but they would have been cold and miserable and tired, and it would have been too easy to wear them down.

He didn't like wasting dragons.

"You'll be all right, Dune," he whispered in his friend's ear as they flew. "We're almost there. They'll fix you and you'll be flying again in no time. Just hang on."

They landed beside the medical tent in the center of camp, and three dragons immediately emerged, clustering around Dune.

"He needs heat on that wound, and fast," Six-Claws said, pointing to the glistening ice crystals and blue-black scales along the edge of Dune's wing. "Do everything you can for him."

"Of course, sir," one of them answered.

"He might lose the foot," said another, studying Dune's damaged foreleg, "but he needs his wings more. We can save those."

"Yes, we can heal injuries like this, sir," said the last one, indicating the frostbreath gently. "We've done it before. It's not too bad."

"Thank you," said Six-Claws. They whisked Dune away into the tent.

Six-Claws wanted to follow, but he couldn't. There was

too much to do. Dragons he had to see and dispatches he needed to read and —

He turned around and found Queen Burn looming behind him.

"Your Majesty," he said with a bow.

"Still alive," she commented.

"Me?" he said. "Yes, I'm afraid so."

"Show me your claws again," she ordered.

He forced himself not to sigh. This happened every time he saw her; he should be over how sick and uncomfortable it made him feel. He held out his front talons.

"Yesssss," Burn hissed, taking them in hers and staring at them greedily. She tugged on his sixth claw on each side and eyed his face to see if he'd react. He kept his expression blank.

"Your soldiers remember their orders, do they?" Burn said. "When you die in battle, they know they are to cut off your arms and bring them to me."

"Yes, Your Majesty," he said. It took all his considerable training to keep still instead of yanking his talons away from her. "They know. They won't forget." How could they forget a gruesome order like that? Everyone knew exactly what she wanted to do with Six-Claws's talons. One day, when he died, she would happily dismember him and preserve his odd-looking claws in her creepy weirdling tower, along with all the other strange and horrible things she'd collected over the years.

Burn finally dropped his talons with a snort. "Well, as long as you're still alive, you'd better make yourself useful. We're going to attack the MudWings. Pack everyone up. We move out tomorrow."

"What?" Six-Claws blurted.

"Don't disappoint me by being deaf and slow as well," she growled. "The MudWings. We're attacking them. As soon as possible." She chuckled. "My spies tell me there's been a rift between the SeaWings and the MudWings. Blister's alliance is falling apart. This is the time to attack! If we strike now, we can intimidate the MudWings into joining *our* side. Then we'll be unstoppable."

"But wait," Six-Claws said. "What about our plan? The whole strategy we worked out?"

"*Your* plan, you mean," said Burn. "I know, I know. Focus our energy here until we find Blaze and kill her, so we only have one enemy instead of two." She yawned. "Boring. You haven't found Blaze yet and I hate waiting."

"We've only been looking for a few weeks," Six-Claws protested. "They're fighting hard to keep her hidden. I'm sure today's battle was close to her hiding spot."

He'd never admitted his secret hope, of course. What he really wanted was for one sister to die so the other two could fight it out — just the two of them in a regular duel, with no armies or soldiers or other tribes or innocent bystanders dragged into the mess. He wanted this to be *over*.

And for that, his strategy made the most sense. If they

kept pounding away at Blaze's IceWing alliance, surely they would find her soon.

"You know," Burn sneered, "if you want Blaze dead so badly, perhaps you shouldn't have saved her life all those years ago." She flicked her tail at the shouts of pain coming from the medical tent. "Maybe all of this is *your* fault."

Six-Claws clenched his talons, trying not to reveal that he'd had that exact thought himself over several sleepless nights.

"Your Majesty," he said as calmly as he could. "I strongly believe that we should stick with our current strategy."

"Well, *I* strongly believe that we should go kill some MudWings," she said. "And *I* am your queen, so that means *I* always win."

"Can we discuss this?" he asked. He didn't want to sound as though he was begging, but maybe that was what she wanted him to do. "I can show you the maps — our deductions — our next steps — we have it all worked out."

"You disloyal worm," Burn snarled. "I can see you need a little extra persuasion." She pushed past him and shoved her way into the medical tent.

He started to follow her, but suddenly there was a hiss from the shadows beside the tent.

"Who's there?" he said, pausing. It was impossible to see past the light of the torches, but he could tell there was a dragon hiding in the dark.

A pause, and then an unfamiliar voice said, "Someone with your best interests at heart."

"Show yourself," Six-Claws ordered. Perhaps it could be one of his soldiers, but he thought he'd recognize all their voices. Was it someone sent by one of Burn's sisters to attack her?

If so, it was bad, it was very, very bad that a part of him was tempted not to stop them.

"You don't have to follow Burn," whispered the voice. "She doesn't deserve it."

"Who should I follow instead?" Six-Claws asked. "I suppose you have someone in mind. Blister?"

"Dear snakes, no," said the hidden dragon, with what sounded like genuine amusement. "Why follow any of them? There's always the Scorpion Den, right? Plenty of SandWings there who don't fight for anyone. From what I've heard anyhow."

"Deserters," Six-Claws said. "That's not me. I'm loyal."

"Loyal to what?" asked the dragon. "Do you even know why you follow her anymore? She's not a good queen. You are helping a viper and making her stronger and more poisonous. Can't you see that?" He paused. "If you can't, you will soon, I'm afraid."

"SIX-CLAWS!" Burn roared from inside the tent. "Get in here!"

"Think about it," the dragon in the shadows whispered, and then he seemed to melt away, and when Six-Claws blinked, there was no one there at all.

He pushed through the flaps into the tent and found Burn standing over Dune.

Six-Claws's friend was lying on a low pile of blankets, unconscious, with his wings spread out on either side of him. Sacks filled with fire-heated stones were packed around the frostbreath injury on his wing and also around his front leg. Here, in the torchlight, Six-Claws could see the wounds more clearly, and he saw that an IceWing must have raked Dune with her serrated claws as well.

But his wing would heal and he would fly again. The doctors said they could fix him. He'd be all right.

"This is the little toad who follows you around, isn't it?" Burn asked. She jabbed one of the hot stone bags so it slid off Dune's wing.

Six-Claws started forward. "He needs that —"

"Don't move," Burn snarled. She pushed another healing pack off the injured dragon, and Dune made a small noise of pain, but didn't wake up. Behind Burn, one of the doctors was wringing her talons like she wanted to intervene but didn't dare.

"Please. Don't hurt him," Six-Claws said, his stomach twisting. "He's a loyal soldier to you."

"And what are you?" Burn demanded. "Tell me, where are we going tomorrow?"

Six-Claws hesitated. He felt as if there was a possible end to this war slipping right between his talons. "I'll do what you say, Your Majesty. I will. But if I could have just one more day to look for Blaze —"

Burn slammed her talons down on Dune's injured wing. Dune came awake screaming as the frozen parts snapped off completely, leaving only misshapen, blackened ruin. Burn sliced her claws through the tendons and membranes, destroying what was left of the wing.

"*No!*" Six-Claws heard himself shouting, felt himself tackled by the other SandWings in the tent as he lunged toward the queen.

"Unquestioning obedience," Burn said to him. "That's really all I ask." She kicked Dune aside and shook the blood off her claws. "So, General. Where are we going tomorrow?"

There were at least three dragons pinning him down. Six-Claws took a deep breath, forcing away his guilt and fury and disbelief. "The Mud Kingdom," he said into the ground.

"Much better." Burn stepped over him, nearly smacking him in the face with her deadly tail. "You're lucky you're such a useful general, or I would just take those fascinating talons for my tower and be done with these boring arguments. Oh, and Six-Claws." She stopped in the opening of the tent and looked back at him. "The next time you feel like questioning my orders, remember that your friend there has another wing . . . and a tail . . . and three working legs, all of which could meet with even more horrible accidents. Understood?"

"Yes, Your Majesty." Six-Claws couldn't look at her. He kept his eyes closed and his face in the sand until he heard her leaving the tent and her heavy footsteps treading away.

"We're sorry, sir," said one of the nurses, climbing off him. "We didn't want her to kill you."

"I understand," he said as they all let go and backed away nervously. He staggered to his feet and over to Dune, who had mercifully passed out again. His wing was a wreck, far beyond saving, and his foreleg was a bloody stump. Six-Claws knelt beside him and gently touched Dune's head. "Is there anything you can do for him?" he asked the other dragons.

They tried. He could see how hard they were trying. He didn't leave Dune's side as they bandaged and swabbed and did what they could. His other duties had all faded into a blur in the back of his mind.

The Scorpion Den.

You are helping a viper.

Think about it.

"It's getting late, sir." One of the doctors brushed Six-Claws's wing with her own. "You should get some sleep."

"I'm not going to sleep," he said. "I'm getting Dune out of here. As far away from *her* as I can get him."

The doctor glanced around and Six-Claws realized they were alone, apart from Dune; the other SandWings had left without him realizing it.

"Where are you going?" she whispered. She was the one who'd thought about stopping Burn; he remembered the horror and pity in her eyes. He'd seen her before, taking care of other patients. She was always calm and efficient. He liked that about her, even though he didn't really know her.

"The Scorpion Den, I think," he whispered back. He rubbed his eyes. "I'll have to carry him."

"I'll help you," she said. "If — if you don't mind me coming with you."

He could use the help — Dune was too heavy to carry far on his own. But he shook his head. "It's too dangerous," he said. "You'd be a deserter, like us. Burn would kill you if she caught you."

"Apparently she might kill me even if I stay right here," the doctor said wryly. "I'd rather go with you. I trust you."

"You don't know me at all," he said.

"Of course I do," she answered. "You're General Six-Claws."

"It'll just be Six-Claws from now on," he said. "I don't know your name."

"Kindle," she said. "Let's go now, before anyone comes back."

They wrapped Dune in blankets and lifted him between them as carefully as they could. Outside, the temperature had dropped to almost freezing, and most dragons were huddled in their tents. No one questioned Six-Claws and Kindle as they carried their burden to the outskirts of the encampment.

"General, sir," said the dragon on guard duty, snapping back her wings as they approached.

"We're taking this dragon back to the stronghold for more advanced medical treatment," Six-Claws said.

"Do you want me to take him?" the soldier offered. "You should rest, shouldn't you, sir?"

"I'll be fine," said Six-Claws. "But thank you."

"Yes, sir," she answered. "I hope he's all right."

Kindle took one side of the blankets and Six-Claws took the other, and with Dune slung between them, they lifted off into the night sky.

I'm sorry to leave you, Six-Claws thought at the soldier on guard duty . . . at all the soldiers he had to leave behind. He felt like the lowest snake in the sandpit, abandoning his position and all the dragons who'd counted on him.

But the dragon in the shadows was right. Six-Claws was helping a monster rise to power, and he couldn't do it anymore. Especially not if it meant Dune would have to live in constant danger.

He'd try to find a way to save the others. Maybe he could get more of them out, anyone who wished to be free of Burn or the other two sisters. Maybe together they could make the Scorpion Den a safe place for dragons who wanted no part of this war.

Dune shifted in the blankets and Six-Claws had to adjust his wingbeats to the way his weight rolled. He glanced down and saw Dune looking up at him with bleak, haunted eyes.

Not at Six-Claws — at his wings, powering steadily through the air. The way Dune's never would again.

"I'm sorry, Dune," Six-Claws said.

Dune didn't respond for a long time. Finally he asked, "Where are we going?"

"To the Scorpion Den," Six-Claws answered. "I'm taking you somewhere I hope Burn will never find us."

"Burn." Dune let out a bitter laugh. "You always said it was so important to be loyal. I guess we've learned something about loyalty, haven't we?"

Six-Claws beat his wings in silence for a moment. "Yes," he agreed at last.

"That it's stupid," Dune said, "and *we* were stupid for being loyal in the first place, and now we're paying for it. I'm paying for it. There's no point to any of this."

"No, that's not it," Six-Claws said. "We were loyal to the wrong dragon, that's all. I see that now."

"Oh, good," Dune said sarcastically, stuffing his nose into the blankets. "Just in time."

"We'll be more cautious in the future," Six-Claws said. The sun was starting to rise off to his left, casting dazzling sunspots in the corners of his eyes. "We'll find a dragon we can truly trust and respect, and then we'll have a reason to be loyal. I believe that dragon exists. You'll see."

"Wonderful," Dune muttered. "Can't wait."

Six-Claws glanced over at Kindle. She was blinking away tears, outlined by the halo of the rising sun.

"I hope you're right," she said.

"Me too," he said, and they flew on together, south toward the Scorpion Den, toward an uncertain future, toward that tiny thread of hope.

WINGS OF FIRE

WINGLETS #4: RUNAWAY

Note: The events of this story take place
immediately after the prologue of Wings of Fire: Legends:
Darkstalker, thousands of years before the events of
Wings of Fire Book One: *The Dragonet Prophecy*.

Snow speckled the black dragon's wings and shoulders. Small chunks of ice were caught between her claws, and she shook her talons to knock them loose before stepping into the tunnel. The smooth, curved channel led to a vast dome made of blocks of more ice, ice upon snow upon frozen ground.

But she wasn't cold.

Foeslayer touched the diamond earring in her ear.

An enchantment just for me.

A dragon who doesn't think I'm a total waste of space.

He'd gone in ahead of her, for the sake of appearances. Her eyes found him immediately as she entered the dome—even in the crowd of IceWings, he glittered the brightest. Not even his mother, Queen Diamond of the IceWings, could outshine him. Moon globes floating near the ceiling cast a cool, pale light that made the IceWings look polished and silvery, but turned the visiting black dragons dull and greenish.

Prince Arctic seemed to be listening raptly to his mother's lecture, but his gaze flickered to Foeslayer for a brief moment. A moment of *I see you*. A moment of *this is torture but I can survive it now that I've met you*. A moment of *you are the only other dragon in the world*.

It took her breath away. The NightWings in her own kingdom never took Foeslayer seriously. She was too scatter-brained, too likely to blurt whatever she was thinking. She got too passionate over things nobody else cared about — like the way visiting merchant RainWings or MudWings were sequestered from the NightWings instead of being invited to their parties and festivals. Her friends sniffed that it served the RainWings right for the exorbitant prices they charged for their fruit, and that MudWings weren't smart enough to be interesting anyway.

No one had ever looked at Foeslayer the way Arctic did — as though being different and a little weird was a good thing. As though it made her fascinating rather than annoying.

"Where have you been?" Her mother was suddenly there, blocking her view of Arctic, briskly brushing the snow off Foeslayer's scales. "You look frightful and you must be freezing. I told you the prince was coming! Didn't I say to stay put in your corner?"

"We're in a dome," Foeslayer pointed out. "It doesn't have corners."

Prudence narrowed her eyes at her daughter. "Foeslayer, don't be a toadstool right now. I don't need your smart mouth ruining everything." She flicked Foeslayer's ear with one of her claws, then stopped and peered at it sharply. Foeslayer winced in anticipation half a second before her mother's claws closed in, pinching the diamond and sending a burst of pain through all the nerves of Foeslayer's skull.

"*Where did this earring come from?*" Prudence snarled.

"Ow, ow, ow." Foeslayer tried to pull away but her mother forced her back into a crouch. "It was a gift, that's all, stop hurting me!"

Prudence let go suddenly with a hiss and jumped back, shaking her talon as though she'd been burned. Maybe she had — Foeslayer felt a glow of heat spreading from the earring. *It's enchanted to keep me safe from danger, too. Even from Mother.*

"You cannot *steal things* from the IceWings," Prudence hissed. "This is shocking even for you, Foeslayer."

"I didn't! An IceWing gave it to me!" Foeslayer protested.

"Which IceWing?" Prudence growled. "I told you not to talk to any IceWings!"

"Is everything all right here?"

Oh, it was bad, a bad, bad terrible thing that her heart leaped at the sound of his voice.

Too bad this earring isn't smart enough to protect me from my own heart.

Prudence whirled and found Arctic standing regally behind her, his eyes cold and unfriendly. He must have almost flown across the dome to get there so quickly. The IceWing queen and a small entourage of aristocrats were hurrying after him.

"Prince Arctic," Prudence said, drawing herself up to look as haughty as he did. "This need not concern you. I am merely chastising my wayward daughter, who seems to have found and kept an earring that does not belong to her." She held out her open talon to Foeslayer with a meaningful glare. "I will make sure she returns it immediately."

"By no means," said the prince. He intercepted Foeslayer's arm as she reached for the earring and pressed it back down to her side. His scales were cool, like running water, and his talons squeezed hers lightly, almost imperceptibly: *I'm here for you.* "I gave her that earring as a token of the forthcoming alliance between our tribes. It would be inexpressibly rude to reject it."

"We met outside," Foeslayer explained to her mother's disbelieving face. "By accident." *Arctic, by all the moons, stop being so obvious. You're going to get me killed.* Prudence wasn't the only one who looked angry. Queen Diamond was within earshot now, and her suspicious eyes stabbed through Foeslayer like icicles.

"I am very sorry my daughter bothered you," Prudence said to Arctic. "Foeslayer, return to our chambers at once."

"Absolutely," Foeslayer agreed, with immense relief. She would really like to be anywhere but here right this moment.

She saw Arctic open his mouth to protest and shot him an extremely stern "shut up" look. "I'll go right now."

"That is what 'at once' means," Prudence said. Her frown deepened as Foeslayer started to back away. "Don't you need this?" she barked, holding up her arm. On her wrist glinted the silvery metal of one of the animus-touched bracelets.

The IceWings had three of these bracelets, each enchanted to protect a dragon from the cold temperatures and defensive weaponry of the Ice Kingdom. Because there were only three, visiting diplomatic parties were craftily kept small and outnumbered at every meeting. And they were also a handy way to remind outsiders about the power of the IceWings' animus magic.

But Foeslayer was an unexpected fourth member of the party. She was supposedly there so her mother could keep an eye on her, although she suspected one of the real reasons was that Queen Vigilance wanted to force the IceWings to reveal that they had a fourth bracelet.

If they did, though, they hadn't produced it yet. So Foeslayer and her mother had to share one between them, meaning Foeslayer would be cold a lot.

Except now she had the earring.

But she couldn't admit that it was magic or what it could do or, most of all, who had enchanted it for her. For one thing, the IceWings had strict rules about animus magic. Prince Arctic was only supposed to use his magic once, in a ceremony to create a gift for his tribe. He certainly wasn't supposed to waste it on an unimportant, scatterbrained NightWing.

"Right," she said to her mother, pretending to shiver. "Yes, please."

"There are blankets in our rooms," Prudence said, dismissing her with a wing flick. "Use those and you'll be fine."

That was typical Mother: She'd act outraged that you didn't want something she was offering, and then as soon as you did want it (or pretended to want it), she'd say you couldn't have it.

Foeslayer couldn't stop herself from rolling her eyes behind Prudence's back. Arctic's gaze was still fixed on her, and she saw him crack a very small smile.

It wasn't quite small enough, though.

Over by the translucent ice wall, another IceWing was staring at them.

Uh-oh.

Her name came back to Foeslayer instantly: Snowflake. *That's Arctic's fiancée,* Foeslayer remembered. *The dragon he's supposed to marry.* The IceWing's expression was impossible to read.

He's taken. It was the first thing Foeslayer had learned about the prince, and yet she'd managed to forget it completely in the magic of meeting him (and in the actual literal magic of him enchanting an earring for her). *He's going to marry someone else.*

But he never could have been mine anyway.

She bowed, turned her back on all the IceWings, and ducked into the tunnel.

So why did I agree to meet him in secret later tonight?

Am I still going to?

A smart dragon wouldn't.

A smart dragon would keep her head down and make it home to the Night Kingdom instead of risking an intertribal incident.

She stepped out into a blizzard that had quietly crept up on them, icy petals blocking out the sky and sea. Near the entrance, she could still see the impression in the snow where Arctic had been standing during their conversation.

Yes, but . . . that smart dragon sounds perfectly miserable.

All right. So what if I choose not to be smart? It's only one secret meeting. I just want to talk to him some more.

I mean, really, universe . . . what's the worst that could happen?

◄─●─►

Snowflake had always suspected that the IceWing royal family was full of snobs, and now that they were here in her parents' palace, she was sure.

Queen Diamond said everything in a superior, condescending tone, peering down her snout as though your ignorance was a grave disappointment to her. She kept making snide comments about the state of the palace and how it could be improved. She never spoke to anyone below the First Circle, and she had clearly chosen Snowflake as her son's fiancée because she thought Snowflake was the quietest option.

(Snowflake knew this because the queen had said it directly to her face. "You're a dragon who knows how to keep her mouth shut," Diamond had mused, gripping Snowflake's chin in her talons to inspect her cheekbones. "Either you understand that I'm not interested in your opinions, or you don't have any, which would be preferable. I suppose I'll be able to tolerate your presence in my palace, so long as you make equally silent brats.")

Frankly, Snowflake had no desire to live in the main IceWing palace, but soon she'd have no choice.

The only time she'd ever been there she'd spent the entire visit in a whirl of tests, competitions, and yet more tests to prove she deserved her place in the First Circle of the IceWing hierarchy. It was infuriating, particularly since many of the tests had been subtle and deliberately unfair — secret traps set by the queen so she could assess Snowflake's strength, poise, diplomacy, and ability to come up with witty rejoinders whenever someone insulted her.

That last wasn't Snowflake's strength. She could do an excellent icy look of disdain, but all the cutting comebacks she should have said only came to her during the night, much too late, while she lay on her ice shelf, fuming.

The truth was she spent a lot of time fuming. It was a little surprising to her that Queen Diamond couldn't sense the rage under her scales. All those years practicing her cool exterior must have paid off. Her parents had certainly drilled it into her over and over again: *Freeze over your anger. Never let anyone see it. Nobody wants to hear about your feelings. Calm and collected on the outside; that's all that matters.*

She wasn't sure how long she could keep it up, though. Especially around her future husband, Prince Arctic, who was the most arrogant, entitled, patronizing, obnoxious, preening, fatheaded son of a walrus she'd ever met.

He acted as though she were barely Seventh Circle, as though she had an obligation to entertain him when he was bored, and as though she had no brains in her head whatsoever.

How can I possibly marry him?

How am I supposed to look at his SMUG PRETENTIOUS FACE every single day for the rest of my life?

How am I going to last even a month without stabbing my claws through his superior eyeballs?

It was supposed to be such an honor to marry into the royal family. Her parents were ecstatic that all their work on her had paid off. Such glories lay ahead! Her dragonets might inherit animus magic! Her daughters would be directly in line for the throne!

First in line to get killed by their horrible grandmother, that is.

But there was nothing Snowflake could do to change her fate. She obviously couldn't disobey her parents and her queen. She couldn't even hint to them that she might not be interested in their plan for her life. She had to be polite to Arctic and bow deeply to his mother; she had to wear the mask of the perfect daughter, apparently forever.

Forever. Until they store my frozen head on the wall of dead royal family members and slide my corpse into the cold ocean.

Forever trapped in the main palace with Arctic and Diamond.

Unless I can find a way out.

She drew back against the wall of the dome, watching Arctic's face as the loudmouthed NightWing left. She'd noticed the dazzled look in his eyes the moment he saw Foeslayer, and it was still there. He'd dismissed Snowflake, his moonsforsaken fiancée, as though she were an inconvenient dragonet underfoot. And then—it must have been only moments later—he'd given Foeslayer his diamond earring.

His *earring*. Of all the sappy *nonsense*. Only characters in very bad, very sentimental scrolls did stuff like that.

He probably thinks he's very romantic.

With the WRONG DRAGON, you moron.

Not that she'd accept any jewelry from him if he offered. The rest of the tribe might find animus magic perfectly wonderful and useful, but Snowflake didn't trust anyone with that kind of power.

"My, my, my," said a voice that slithered like seals worming across a patch of ice. "Wasn't that an interesting interaction."

Snowflake swiveled her head around to face the approaching IceWing: female, slightly older than Snowflake, not from this palace, wearing a First Circle necklace. She was white with a scattering of gray-blue scales that looked like rippling shadows across her wings, and she moved like a confident predator.

Snowflake dipped her head in a polite half bow, wondering where their names each ranked on the wall and whether she should be bowing deeper. "Please accept my apologies, for I do not recognize your face," she said. "I hope I am not bringing great dishonor upon my family." That was one of the stock phrases she'd learned very young, designed to help dragonets wriggle out of awkward situations.

"No, we haven't met yet," said the new dragon, nodding back in a way that suggested her rank was higher. "I'm Snowfox."

Oh, thought Snowflake. *Queen Diamond's niece.* She'd certainly heard of this dragon, currently the only living heir to the IceWing throne.

Snowfox smiled, and tiny embedded gems glittered from her teeth. "Snowfox and Snowflake — we're either destined to be great friends or terrible enemies, aren't we? Let's avoid any confusion; you may call me Fox."

"Certainly, as long as you never call me Flake," Snowflake said, smiling back.

Fox laughed. "I'm sure you're anything but," she said. "It must take a very cunning dragon to ensnare the talons of

Prince Arctic." Her dark blue eyes cut toward the remaining NightWings, her brows lifting innocently.

"I promise you, the only cunning dragon involved in this plan is the queen," Snowflake answered, ignoring Fox's implication. "I take no credit for the match."

"Then true love with a handsome prince just fell into your talons?" Fox said slyly. "You must be the happiest dragon in the Ice Kingdom."

"I am so lucky," Snowflake agreed, letting the faintest whiff of sarcasm creep into her tone. "He's very . . . charming."

They both watched Arctic for a silent moment. Now that Foeslayer was gone, he had lapsed back into what appeared to be his usual sullen mood, grunting and scowling at everything anyone said to him.

"I'm sure there are many other dragons who would love to be in your scales," Fox said, shooting another sideways glance at the NightWing delegation.

"Naturally," Snowflake said. "Who wouldn't want to marry a prince and watch her daughters fight to the death for the throne?"

"Well," said Fox. "True love. Right?"

"Indeed," said Snowflake. "True love."

Arctic snatched the last bright green drink from a passing tray and stared into it gloomily.

"He's contemplating his noble reflection in the ice cubes," Snowflake observed.

Fox clapped her talons around her own snout, but couldn't hold back a snort so loud that several dragons turned to wrinkle their foreheads at her.

"Silvery moons," she said when she'd recovered the power of speech and everyone was ignoring them again. "You have a depth of dark water below your ice, don't you?"

"Only for my greatest friends . . . and most terrible enemies," Snowflake replied, meeting Fox's eyes.

"Now I'm quite sure which one I'd rather be." Fox tipped her head, calculating. After a long moment, she said, "Do you know what will happen if you *don't* end up having daughters with Prince Arctic?"

"I miss out on the tremendous fun of watching my mother-in-law rip them apart?" Snowflake guessed.

"That," said Fox. "Also, only one dragon is left to challenge Diamond for the throne."

Snowflake looked at her, realization dawning. "You."

Fox tipped her head down modestly. "Me."

"It seems," Snowflake said slowly, "that you and I have some mutual goals."

"Isn't it wonderful to meet a dragon who's a kindred spirit?" Fox said. She draped her tail lightly over Snowflake's and leaned a little closer, her odd looks tipping over into beautiful inside Snowflake's mind.

A dragon who understands me, finally. A dragon as deep and dark as I am, who sees my anger and wants to be nearer to it instead of freezing it away.

"I have a few ideas . . . if you're interested," said Fox.

"Whatever you have to say," Snowflake said, "I'll always be listening."

The two IceWings bent their heads together, whispering, as the gale built into a howling snowstorm outside.

–◆●◆–

Snow drifted through the window, gathering softly along the sill and feathering the floor. The sky outside was dark, and the silver flakes looked as if they were whirling up out of a deep abyss.

Prince Arctic stared into that abyss, thinking that it looked an awful lot like his future.

Pinned under Mother's claws for the rest of my life. Unable to use my own magic after the gifting ceremony. Married to Snowflake, who hates me.

Never seeing Foeslayer again.

How could he bear it?

How could this be all he'd ever have of happiness—nine days of secret meetings, and then nothing more for the rest of his life?

Snowflake had become more unfriendly with each passing day, responding to him with the barest minimum of chilly conversation. It was almost like someone—the great ice dragon, the universe, whoever—wanted to make it very clear how different Snowflake and Foeslayer were.

Because Foeslayer . . . she was sunlight and all the moons and the whole star-filled sky. He'd met her only nine days ago but already she was the beginning and end of his universe. She made him laugh—had anyone else ever done that? She made him want to be warm. She made him brave and careless; she made him forget about circles and walls and protocol and ranks and rules.

She made him a dragon he actually wanted to be.

But she was leaving.

The day after tomorrow, the NightWings would be escorted over the Great Ice Cliff and their protective bracelets would be removed. Foeslayer would fly south and out of his life, while Arctic flew north with his mother and the royal guard. Home to the main palace, to prepare for his gifting ceremony.

Tonight would be the second-to-last time he'd be able to sneak off and see her alone. Tonight, tomorrow night, and then never again.

It had been difficult to find a safe time to meet. The NightWings normally slept all day, while the IceWings slept at night, like normal dragons. But for the purposes of this visit, the NightWings had shifted their schedule over, waking in the late afternoon so they could negotiate with the queen and dine with her court in the evenings, and then going to bed in the early morning when it was still dark outside. So there was a small window of time when everyone (except the night watch guards) was asleep, and that was when Arctic and Foeslayer met, in the stolen moments before dawn.

Arctic brushed a tiny pile of snow into his talons and stared at it, thinking of how snowflakes like these melted when they touched Foeslayer's scales.

A strange feeling crept over him . . . a crawling sensation between his wings . . . a sense of being watched.

He whirled around.

His mother stood in the doorway, filling the frame like a glacier that had swept in from the mountains, crushing everything in its path. Ice-blue diamonds cascaded from her ears and around her neck and all along her tail band, but none of them glittered as sharply or as dangerously as her eyes.

Arctic wanted to ask how long she'd been standing there, but of course, instead, he bowed deeply. He imagined Foeslayer yelping, "Official creepiest queen in Pyrrhia!" and was glad he had a moment with his head down so he could compose his face.

"Sssson," Diamond hissed. "Why are you awake at this hour?"

Arctic arranged his wings and head in the approved talking-to-the-queen position. "I couldn't sleep, Your Majesty." *Why are YOU awake? Are you spying on me? Do you know something?*

"That sounds very undisciplined," she rumbled, her gaze traveling around the room. "The tribe has strict sleep schedules for a reason. If you have been disrupting yours — as I suspected after I caught you yawning during our breakfast with Snowflake and her parents—then I will assign a chronologer to fix you."

"With gratitude and respect," Arctic said, feeling absolutely none of either, "may I humbly observe that my trouble sleeping seems likely to be related to my gifting ceremony, and therefore is sure to be temporary."

"I didn't lose sleep over *my* gifting ceremony." Diamond slithered across the floor toward him, her claws leaving furrows in the ice. "Which strain of weakness plagues you? Cowardice? Indecision? Wild fantasies of making different choices?"

That last one was a little too close to the truth. Arctic held his eyes steady; his expression unreadable; his answer, silence.

"A true IceWing would not have any such troubles," Diamond said. She loomed over him as though she could read guilt in each of his scales. "I've told you what your gift should be. Obey without question, and you have nothing to fear. Then you will sleep like a loyal IceWing—deeply, and at the appropriate assigned times."

Arctic didn't trust himself to speak. His mind echoed with the sound of Foeslayer laughing, two nights ago, as he playfully wrapped a curtain around her snout to muffle the noise. She'd pushed him away, giggling, and freed herself.

"Seriously, explain this so it actually makes sense," she'd said. "Your mother wants you to make a what?"

"A bowl of ice—or a moon globe, or a mirror would be acceptable—that much I'm allowed to decide, apparently."

"With the power to . . . ?"

". . . predict the weather," he'd admitted.

"That's it?"

"Well—to predict it pretty far in advance, mind you. At least a year ahead."

"Um, I can predict your weather a year in advance. It's going to . . . wait for it . . . oh, this is pretty shocking . . . it's going to SNOW! And then a couple of days later . . . you're not going to believe it . . . snow again! And then, wait, this one's a bit tricky . . . hang on to your tails, everyone . . . it looks like we're in for about three hundred and sixty-five more days of . . . great moons! MORE SNOW!"

"Stop making me laugh! I'm going to end up with weird little laugh wrinkles around my eyes and no one in the Ice Kingdom will know what they are."

"I like your weird little laugh wrinkles."

"I like your weird little way you mispronounce words."

"I BEG your pardon. YOU'RE the one who says things all squonkily."

"That's not a word at all. And incidentally, sometimes our snow comes in the form of a raging terrible blizzard, which would be quite useful to know about ahead of time, thank you very much."

"But come on," Foeslayer had said, rolling her eyes. "How can she call that a 'gift of vision'? Is there anything less visionary you could do with your powers? Don't listen to her, Arctic. It's your magic. Make something completely wonderful with it."

"Yeah?" he'd said. "Like what?"

"Well — if you really want a 'gift of vision,' why not have it show more of the future than the weather? Like, who the next queen of the SkyWings is going to be, or how the dispute along the Great Five-Tail River will be resolved, or where the best veins of silver and diamond mines can be found? You could make it see the future or answer any question you ask it or show you any dragon on the continent or literally ANYTHING more interesting than the weather."

Arctic had stared at her.

"Ooo, I love that face," she'd said. "That's your 'I wish I'd thought of that!' face! I know you do. Don't feel bad; I'm just way smarter than you."

"You aggravating moonhead —"

"Here's the thing, though," she'd interrupted him — no one interrupted him! "Don't actually do that, because if you enchant it to see the future or answer any question, then the queen will be able to find out who kills her to become the next queen. And I'm pretty sure she'll straight-up murder that granddaughter in her egg." She'd hesitated. "Your daughter," she'd added softly.

Arctic's imaginary future as a father having dragonets with Snowflake had never felt less real, less possible.

"Do you have any other ideas for animus gifts?" he'd asked.

"Only about eighty million!" she'd said. "Do you want to hear them all? Feel free to take notes in case your brain gets tired."

"Listen, NightWing, don't you know you're not supposed to talk to princes that way?"

"I think there's a lot of things we're both doing right now that we're not supposed to," she'd pointed out, sweeping her wing around the alcove where they were hiding.

"Like falling in love?" he'd asked, taking her talons in his.

"Now that," she'd whispered back, "is something you're definitely, absolutely not supposed to say."

"Arctic!" Queen Diamond barked.

He jumped, and realized with a rush of terror that he hadn't been holding his expression still while the memory washed over him. What had Diamond seen in his face in that unguarded moment? Could she guess what it meant?

"I asked you a question," she said, her voice brimming with outrage.

Oh, worse and worse. "My deepest apologies," he said, bowing low again. "Perhaps I am more tired than I thought and should go to sleep at once."

"Answer it first," she snapped. "Do you swear to give the tribe the gift of vision as I described it to you?"

He hesitated. It was dangerous and unheard of to contradict her—his parent and his queen—but if he lied and said yes, she'd be even more furious when he disobeyed her at the gifting ceremony itself.

"I have another idea," he said cautiously. "I was hoping to discuss it with you. Perhaps in the morning?" He had to get rid of her. Foeslayer must be in their spot by now, waiting. She'd wonder why he wasn't there.

She wouldn't come looking for me here, would she? he thought with another bolt of fear. She was just bold enough and reckless enough to make such a mistake. And if Diamond saw a NightWing appear in her son's doorway in the middle of the night . . . someone wouldn't survive till dawn.

"Another idea?" said the queen. "One of your own? I don't like the sound of that. Very well, you may present it to me first thing in the morning."

She stalked toward the hall as Arctic breathed a stifled sigh of relief. In a moment she'd be gone, and then he could run to Foeslayer, warn her, and send her flying back to her room as fast as possible.

Queen Diamond stopped in the doorway and gave Arctic a merciless, piercing look. "To make sure that you *do* sleep," she said, "and that you wake at the precisely correct time in order to attend our appointment, I will leave these two guards here inside your door." She flicked her tail out into the hall, and two large IceWing soldiers slipped inside. Big, burly, stone-faced. Not to be argued with, bribed, or tricked. A wall of indestructible ice between him and Foeslayer.

"That's not—" Arctic started, then bit back the rest of his sentence as his mother hissed at him.

"In fact," she spat, "since you are so overwhelmed by this animus gift decision, it seems best for you to stay in seclusion until it is time for the ceremony. Clearly something here has been distracting you, but we won't let that be a problem anymore."

Arctic's heart fell, spinning away into the abyss with the snow.

"Obedience," Queen Diamond said. "Discipline. Order. Strength. And knowing your place. These are the hallmarks of a true IceWing. Don't you ever forget it again, Arctic."

She swept away, leaving Arctic cut off from the dragon he loved forever.

— ● —

Snowflake felt Fox's tail curl around hers, their spikes clicking together.

"Did you hear all that?" Fox whispered.

It was windy and snowy on the balcony across from Arctic's room, but always deserted after dark, and a perfect spot to keep an eye on his movements all night. They'd been watching him sneak off to meet with Foeslayer every night at about this time, but seeing the queen sweep through like a blizzard was a shock.

"How did she know?" Snowflake whispered back. "If her plan for him works, then ours is ruined."

"We won't let that happen," Fox said, squeezing

Snowflake's talon. "You will never have to marry him. I swear by the eggs that hatched the world." She shook the snow off her snout and glanced across at Arctic's shadowy door. "Maybe we were thinking too small anyway. If they were caught together, yes, there would be a scandal, and he would be dishonored, and your parents might let you back out of the marriage. But they might not — they might cover it up somehow. He's still an animus, which makes him valuable, even if Diamond has to kill a quartet of NightWings to clean up his mess." She tapped her chin thoughtfully.

"We need him out of the kingdom," Snowflake suggested. "Or dead. Otherwise someone else will marry him and have dragonets. I haven't forgotten that we're here to solve your problem, too."

"Yours first," said Fox. "Yours is more urgent. I can deal with dragonets later if I have to."

Snowflake smiled and brushed a stray ice crystal from Fox's cheek. Fox hadn't approached Snowflake looking for an ally. Fox had been hoping to sow discord and mistrust between Snowflake and Arctic for her own purposes.

But everything was different now that they knew each other. Fox wanted to protect Snowflake with a fierceness that matched Snowflake's own desire to get Fox on the throne.

A dragon I would do anything for. That's something I never thought I'd see.

"Out of the kingdom," Fox echoed suddenly. "Do you think . . . is he stupid enough to run away with her?"

"If he's not," Snowflake said, "can we *make* him that stupid?"

"He'd have to use his magic to get past those two guards," said Fox.

"And to get her safely away from here," said Snowflake. "Would he risk his soul that way?"

"Risk his soul *and* break the IceWings' strictest rule about animus power. He's a rule follower. I haven't seen any sign of secret courage in him before."

"Neither have I. And for something like this . . . he'd have to break a lot of rules."

Fox flicked her wings back. "He'd have to be desperate."

What would make me desperate? Snowflake thought for a moment, then said slowly, "He'd have to think she was in danger."

"Yes," Fox breathed.

"I can do that," Snowflake said. "Queen Diamond will let me visit him tomorrow, even if no one else can. I'll hint to him that the queen is displeased with the turn the negotiations have taken."

"He'll believe that," Fox observed, "because it's true. Those NightWings are as arrogant as Diamond. It's almost funny to see which side can stick their snouts higher in the air."

"Yes, this proposed alliance was never going to work."

Snowflake hunched her wings against a gust of wind. "I could have told them that from the beginning."

"So when he hears that the queen is angry with them . . ."

"Then I'll hint that the queen might have other, deadlier plans for the NightWings . . . especially for one of them."

"And he'll believe *that*," said Fox, "because Diamond was acting like she knew all about his secret romance tonight. Whether she really does know or not, he'll find it easy to imagine that she might kill his dear moon-eyed truly beloved out of vengeance or spite."

"Or to make sure she's out of his life forever." Snowflake nodded. "It will be almost too easy to slip those worries into his mind after tonight."

"You're brilliant," said Fox, tossing her wings wide and spinning on the balcony, letting the snow whirl around her. "And meanwhile, I'll spread a rumor among the guards that something strange might be happening tomorrow night. If they see Arctic trying to escape with the NightWings, he won't be able to change his mind and slither back. He'll have to keep flying."

"Don't let Queen Diamond find out, though," Snowflake said. "She needs to sleep through it, or else she could use her magic to stop them."

"No fear," said Fox. "She'll miss the whole thing. In fact, I might have a sleeping potion I bought from a RainWing once that could be useful . . ."

"*You're* brilliant," said Snowflake.

"I hope the guards won't be cowards," Fox said, looking out at the whirling snowflakes. "I want to make sure Arctic doesn't get past us without a fight."

"I want to be there, too," said Snowflake. "I want to see his face when he realizes he's not the great ice dragon's gift to the world after all. When he discovers we've outsmarted him."

"And if something goes wrong," said Fox, making an innocently sad face, "and he doesn't make it . . . or they both don't make it . . ."

"Well," said Snowflake, "that wouldn't be the end of the world either."

◆●◆

Snow, endless snow, snow as far as the edge of the universe, snow forever; snow in her nose and between her claws and melting into her scales and sticking to her talons and weighing down her wings; snow on the rooftops, burying the palace, covering the world; snow everywhere, always falling, always underfoot, always sneaking through the windows and under the blankets and WHY WAS THERE SO MUCH MOON-SPLATTING SNOW?

"I hate this kingdom," Foeslayer offered, pacing up and down the small room again.

"Really," said Prudence drily. She was rolling blankets and packing their belongings, preparing for their departure in the morning. "That's surprising. You've been acting obnoxiously cheerful since we got here."

"I . . . liked being away from court," Foeslayer said. "But I don't know how anyone can *live* like this. I bet having snow in their faces all the time is what makes them so grumpy. Their boring landscapes and no fire anywhere and creepy floating lights. I bet it turns them *all* into total jerks."

Prudence gave her a strange look and Foeslayer realized she should probably shut up.

But he *was* a jerk. How could he not show up, when he knew she was leaving? Had all his pretty sparkly words been lies? Did he always flirt with strange dragons who visited his kingdom and then drop them without saying good-bye?

I know it had to be good-bye. But couldn't we at least have that?

And then he hadn't appeared at any of the final farewell gatherings or the last feast. Foeslayer's mother thought he was snubbing them, "typical IceWing prince." Foeslayer had worried that he was sick, or that something terrible had happened.

But then she managed to casually fly by his window, and he was in there, looking JUST FINE, eating little fish cakes with SNOWFLAKE. Like he'd already forgotten about her. Like he could just go back to normal and carry on with his life, as though nothing had happened at all.

JUST FINE.

Her pacing slowed for a moment, and she reached up to touch her earring. But *this* was real. He'd broken the rules and used his magic and risked his soul for her. So it all had to be real, didn't it?

Arrrrrrrrrrrrrrrrrrrrrrrrrrrrrrrrrrgh.

"Foeslayer, you are driving me mad," said Prudence. "Either sit in a corner and read or help me pack. If I hear your claws squeaking back and forth on the ice one more time, I'll remove—"

Prudence abruptly fell silent.

Foeslayer turned from the window to look at her.

The older NightWing stood frozen, her mouth open as if she might continue the sentence any moment. Her eyes were blank, her talons unmoving. She held a blanket half-folded in her claws.

"Mother?" Foeslayer said, approaching her. "Are you all right?" She poked her mother's wing and got no reaction. "Mother?"

"Sorry," said a voice behind her.

Foeslayer whirled and found Arctic's head sticking out of the wall. She let out a little shriek before she could stop herself.

"She'll be all right," Arctic said. His shoulders, wings, and front talons slipped through the wall, followed by the rest of him. "I did it to the guards in my room, too. It'll wear off in a few hours, once we're far enough away." He held up a tiny dagger with a smile. "Isn't that funny? Mother trusted our rules so much she left two ordinary dragons to guard an animus. As if I couldn't make myself a cool magic thing to get out of there. As if I wouldn't *dare*."

"You just walked through a wall!" Foeslayer cried.

"Oh," said Arctic, tapping one of his armbands. "That's only a little spell. It can do this, too." He turned it clockwise around his arm and vanished into thin air.

"Whoa," said Foeslayer. She reached out toward the space where he'd been and felt invisible talons clasp hers.

"Now you are, too," he whispered. She looked down and realized with a shiver that she couldn't see herself anymore.

"That's a lot of magic," she said, glancing over at Prudence. "You shouldn't have wasted your magic just to come say good-bye to me. I mean, I'm glad you did, but—"

"I'm not saying good-bye," he said. "I refuse to say good-bye to you."

Foeslayer's traitorous heart leaped. "But you have to," she said.

"*No*." He became visible again, turning the armband back the other way. "I don't want to live without you. Foeslayer, let's run away together. We can find an island to hide on! Or maybe the stories of the lost continent are true . . . We must be able to find somewhere we can be safe, and, more importantly, be together."

Can we? Could it really be possible?

"What about your mother's magic?" she asked. "She'll be

so furious—what if she decides to use it? Won't she be able to find us anywhere we go?"

"I have magic, too," he said. "I can hide us from her. You don't have to be afraid." He reached out and touched Foeslayer's earring gently with one claw. "As long as she is wearing it, I enchant this earring to forever keep Foeslayer safe from any enchantment Diamond might cast."

How could I not fall in love with a dragon who wraps all his magic in his love for me?

Maybe they could do it. Maybe they could escape and be happy, secretly, just the two of them, far away from their overbearing mothers and stifling royal courts.

It was so tempting . . . except . . .

Foeslayer looked over at the scowling statue of Prudence. She wasn't a great mother, but she was still *her* mother.

"If we run away," Foeslayer said, "your mother will kill mine, and the other two NightWings as well. She'll think I convinced you to run off with me and she'll blame them. If she can't reach me, she'll need a target for her anger, and they'll be right here, in her claws."

"So I'll give them protection spells, too," Arctic said, sounding frustrated. He lifted one shoulder in a careless shrug.

"No, save your magic," Foeslayer said, although what she really meant was *save your soul*. "We have to take them with us. We escape, all of us, right now."

"Take them with us?" Arctic said, recoiling a little. "I

wasn't exactly picturing your mother in our secret romantic hideout."

Foeslayer brushed his wing with hers. "We don't have to go looking for an island that might not exist and then be fugitives forever. Come to the Night Kingdom. They might be a little mad with me at first, but my tribe will protect you. *I* will protect you."

Arctic let out a little snort that made her bristle. Didn't he think she could protect him? Maybe she didn't have magic, but she was one of the strongest fighters in her class. There were different ways to take care of someone.

"But I'll be the only IceWing there," he said. "And you all sleep in the daytime and live in canyons and who knows what other weird stuff."

"You'll adjust," Foeslayer said, rolling her eyes. "It's a great kingdom; you'll see. And we can get used to anything as long as we're together, right? That's what's important?"

"Yeeeess," he said, a little more reluctantly than she would have liked.

"So it's settled. We'll all fly back to the Night Kingdom tonight," she said.

He hesitated, glancing out at the falling snow.

"Arctic . . . I can't leave them here to die," she said, waving her wing at Prudence. "I'm not that kind of dragon."

Arctic sighed heavily. He pointed the dagger at Prudence and hissed, "Unfreeze."

"—them and give them to the library as quills," Prudence

finished. Her mouth caught up to her eyes, and her jaw dropped at the sight of the IceWing prince standing in her room, his tail twined with Foeslayer's.

"What—" she sputtered. "This—what are you—?"

"There's no time to argue, Mother," Foeslayer said, lifting her chin. "Prince Arctic and I have fallen in love, and he's coming back to the Night Kingdom with us. But that means we have to leave right now."

"Foeslayer!" Prudence exploded. "This is exactly the kind of brainless catastrophe I should have expected from you! But worse! You cannot steal the prince of the IceWings!"

"I'm not stealing him!" Foeslayer protested. "It was his idea! He wants to come with us!"

"More or less," Arctic muttered. "NightWing," he snapped as Prudence opened her mouth again. "You can't stop us. Either you come with us now or I freeze you again, and you can explain all this to my mother in the morning." He brandished the dagger, wagging the tip back and forth.

Muscles clenched all through Prudence's face, as though she were fighting back several waves of rage.

"Fine," she spat suddenly. "I'll get Starclaws and Discretion."

Foeslayer couldn't believe it. She'd expected much more yelling, disapproval, and abuse before her mother gave in. *Maybe there's a small part of her that does want me to be happy,* she thought hopefully.

"I'll scout ahead and freeze any guards in our way," Arctic said. He darted into the hall, leaving Prudence and Foeslayer alone.

"Thank you, Mother," Foeslayer said fervently. "I didn't mean for this to happen, but we just fell in love and he's so wonderful and you'll love him once you get to know him—"

"I knew you were being an idiot," Prudence snapped. "But I let it go on because I hoped you might be enough of an idiot to go home and have his eggs. By then we'd be far enough away that the IceWing queen didn't have to know, and with any luck we'd end up with animus dragons of our own."

Foeslayer faltered. "You . . . you knew?"

"Of course I knew." Prudence snarled softly. "Why do you think I brought you in the first place? You're the only NightWing in the tribe who would do something this idiotic, and I had a feeling you'd catch the prince's eye. But I didn't think *he* was as big an idiot as you are. I thought *he* had some loyalty to his tribe. Some sense of right and wrong. Young dragons are so useless." She stepped toward the door, then spun back to glare at Foeslayer. "All I can say is you'd better have dragonets fast, Foeslayer. As many as possible, so our tribe can inherit animus magic and make this whole disaster worthwhile."

Her mother hurried away toward the rooms of the other two NightWings.

I thought I was doing this great, daring, magical, romantic thing . . . but instead I was walking straight into one of my mother's traps.

Shock reverberated along Foeslayer's wings. She felt as though she'd been dropped into the iciest part of the ocean.

I can never tell Arctic. If he thought we ensnared him deliberately . . . he'd never believe I didn't know. He'd never forgive me.

The IceWing prince slipped back into the room, grinning now from ear to ear. "Coast is clear," he whispered. "I froze the eight guards I found between here and the closest balcony." He flipped the dagger between his claws. "So this is what it feels like to unshackle my power," he said with a laugh. "No wonder the tribe doesn't allow it. I feel so *free*."

"Don't let yourself get too free, though," Foeslayer said. His grin faded and she whisked over to throw her wings around him. "No, keep smiling. I know you're doing all this for me. It'll all be worth it. Together forever, Arctic! We're going to be the happiest dragons in the world."

"We are," he said, holding her close. "But first we have to get out of here."

In the hall they found the other NightWings waiting. Starclaws and Discretion looked a little dazed, but they came along quietly, all of them following Arctic as he slipped stealthily through the dark corridors. Foeslayer's heart twitched with fear when she saw a shape loom up ahead, but it turned out to be one of the frozen guards, staring straight ahead into space. They crept past seven more of them, each IceWing immobile, no longer a threat.

Finally they reached a balcony that faced south, with nothing but open sky and empty land stretching ahead of them, all the way to the dark shadow of the Great Ice Cliff that crossed the horizon.

They stopped on the threshold and Foeslayer saw Arctic take a deep breath. She reached out and wound her tail around his reassuringly.

Please don't change your mind, she prayed. *Don't make me go home alone after this.*

He looked at her, and with her night vision she could see that his expression was unsure. He had imagined a daring flight with only her, an escape from everything they hated. He hadn't imagined giving himself to the NightWings — exchanging one disapproving tribe for another.

"Well, *I'm* going," Prudence said abruptly. "I have no intention of dying for Foeslayer's mistakes." She pushed past Foeslayer and Arctic and launched herself off the edge. Starclaws and Discretion leaped after her.

"Together," Foeslayer said to Arctic.

"Forever," he said slowly.

"Halt! Stop right there!" Six IceWing guards came plummeting out of the night sky, all with diamond-tipped spears strapped to their backs.

"Let's go," Foeslayer cried. She seized Arctic's talons and

dragged him off the balcony. Their wings tangled for a moment, and then they righted themselves, beating furiously as they lifted away. Foeslayer felt the rush of wind swoop past as the IceWings missed them, twisted in the air, and gave chase.

"Prince Arctic?" one of the guards called, confusion weaving through his voice.

For a moment, Arctic faltered beside Foeslayer. "I know that guard," he said when she tugged him forward again. "He was my trainer — he taught me everything I know about weapons."

"It's the NightWings!" screamed a voice from the parapet above them. "They're stealing our prince! *Stop them!*"

Foeslayer glanced back and saw two more IceWings launch themselves from the parapet. The one that was shouting had odd shadowy scales rippling across her pure-white wings, and the other — no, that couldn't be Snowflake, could it?

Whoever it was, the guards were listening. Their wingbeats got stronger, more powerful, and they all drew weapons.

"Keep flying," Foeslayer said breathlessly, pushing Arctic forward. An arrow shot by her snout, barely missing her ear.

"Leave us alone!" Arctic shouted at the guards. "Go back! Let us go!"

Another arrow nearly nicked Foeslayer's wing and she yelped with fear. *The earring will protect me,* she reminded herself, trying to calm her racing heart. *It won't let them hurt me. Just keep flying, Arctic. We just have to stay ahead of them.*

"Stop shooting at her!" Arctic roared.

"We'll save you, Prince Arctic!" called the voice of his teacher.

This time it was a small hail of arrows, but they swerved around Foeslayer's scales.

"I'm all right," she shouted. "Arctic, just keep flying!"

Perhaps Arctic didn't hear her or perhaps he'd forgotten about the earring's protection or perhaps he was too upset by the sight of Foeslayer in danger to think clearly.

Whatever made him do it, Arctic spun in the air, flung his wings open, thrust his front talons toward the pursuing guards, and shouted, "Spears! Stop those guards!"

Foeslayer grabbed his arm in horror. "Arctic, no!"

But it was too late. The spears snapped free — out of the guards' claws or off their backs — pivoted, and stabbed into the IceWings' chests.

"No, wait!" Arctic yelled. "Don't kill them!" He shook his talons frantically and tried to point at the guards again. "Don't kill them! Just stop them, that's all I meant! Leave them alive!"

It was too late. One by one, the six IceWings fell from the sky, dropping like the rocks Foeslayer used to throw into the deepest canyons of the Night Kingdom.

"No!" Arctic cried. "Go back and leave them alive! I

take it back!" He turned to Foeslayer, clutching her arms desperately. "I didn't mean to! I just wanted them to leave us alone!"

"I know," she said. "I know, I know, Arctic, but we have to keep flying. You can't go back now. And those other two are still right behind us."

The two from the wall had caught up to the spot where the IceWings fell, and Foeslayer realized with relief that neither of them had weapons on them—nothing they could attack with, nothing they could be hurt by.

"What did you do?" one of them yelled. She flew toward them and Foeslayer saw that it really was Snowflake, after all. *Why is she even awake? How did she happen to be there as we escaped?*

"You monster!" Snowflake cried, diving at Arctic. "I knew those dragons! How could you just *kill* them? For a *NightWing*? What is *wrong with you*?" She slashed her talons at his snout, but Foeslayer jumped in the way and shoved her back.

"I was going to let you have him," Snowflake shouted at her. "But he doesn't deserve to live! He doesn't deserve to be happy!"

She flew at Arctic again. Foeslayer shot a blast of fire to drive her back—at least, that was what she intended to do.

But at the same moment, she saw Arctic lift his claws, as though he were catching her fireball in his talons, and then shoved it forcefully toward Snowflake.

Fire caught all along one of Snowflake's wings.

At first, Foeslayer thought Snowflake's scream was echoing in her own mind, before she realized the other IceWing was screaming, too. Snowflake's companion plummeted down to catch Snowflake before she could fall to the ground. Frostbreath shot from her mouth, extinguishing the flames, but leaving a trail of blackened marks. Snowflake howled with pain, clutching at her friend as her injured wing flailed uselessly.

"Oh, Arctic," Foeslayer said, her voice catching in her throat. "We have to go. Let's go. Come on, just keep flying. Don't look back."

She dragged him along with her, forcing him to fly. The unfamiliar IceWing started yelling curses after them.

"I'll never forgive you for this!" she roared. "I'll kill every last NightWing if I get a chance! You'll wake up one day with my claws in your eyes! I'm going to wipe out your whole tribe and leave you until last so you'll know their deaths are *all your fault*!"

"Did I kill her?" Arctic asked hoarsely.

"No," said Foeslayer. "Snowflake was hurt, but I'm sure she's still alive." *She may never fly again . . . but he doesn't need to know that.*

They flew in silence until they found Prudence waiting near the Great Ice Cliff.

"I suppose you need this to get across," she said gruffly to Foeslayer, holding up one of the enchanted bracelets that had gotten them safely into the kingdom in the first place.

Foeslayer felt a pang of guilt. *We might not be stealing their prince, but we are stealing their "gift of diplomacy." Will they ever trust another tribe in their kingdom again?*

She thought of the falling, dying guards. *I thought we could escape without anyone getting hurt.*

But the IceWings will hate us forever for this.

"Thank you for waiting, Mother," she said. She touched her earring. "But this will get me across safely."

Prudence squinted at the earring, then threw a sharp look at Arctic. Foeslayer could almost read her mind. She was thinking that if the prince was willing to use his magic like that, maybe he could be convinced to do something useful for the NightWings as well.

Foeslayer felt her throat closing with dread. Poor Arctic, flying right into the tribe's web.

But they'd still be together. That would make up for whatever any other dragons did to them, or how hard life might be . . . wouldn't it?

They soared over the cliff and joined the other two NightWings on the far side. Together they flew south, dipping into the dark clouds that were gathering up ahead.

Foeslayer and Arctic flew near the back, close together, but he didn't say anything for a long, long time.

Foeslayer risked a glance at Arctic's face. He looked as though he'd been stabbed through the heart himself.

"Are you . . . all right?" she asked.

"Obviously not," he snapped back.

She blinked. "I mean—I know you're upset. But I meant, how does your soul feel? Is it OK?"

"My soul is none of your concern," he hissed.

"Um, yes, it is," Foeslayer retorted. "If I'm going to marry you, your soul is very much my concern."

Arctic let out a growl and turned his head away from her.

At the same moment, Prudence turned to glance back at them, and the look on her face was so smug that Foeslayer wished she could claw it right off.

You think you know everything about me and Arctic, Mother. You think we're already falling apart and you're so pleased with yourself. You can't wait to say I told you so *to me every day for the rest of my life.*

But I love Arctic. I do, and that's real. I'm going to make this marriage work. I'm going to make him keep loving me, and I'm not going to let him get away with acting like a jerk. I'm going to hang on to his soul. I'm going to make him happy. We are going to be happy.

Maybe this isn't exactly the fate either of us expected. But it's ours now.

Me and Arctic.

Together against the world.

Forever.

DISCOVER WHERE IT ALL BEGAN . . .

WINGS OF FIRE
LEGENDS
DARKSTALKER

ARCTIC

"Prince Arctic?"

A silvery white dragon poked her head around the door, tapping three times lightly on the ice wall. Arctic couldn't remember her name, which was the kind of faux pas his mother was always yelling at him about. He was a *prince*; it was his *duty* to have all the noble dragons *memorized* along with their *ranks* so he could treat them according to exactly where they fit in the hierarchy.

It was *stupid* and *frustrating* and if his mother yelled at him about it *one more time*, he would seriously enchant something to freeze her mouth shut forever.

Oooo. What a beautiful image. Queen Diamond with a chain of silver circles wound around her snout and frozen to her scales. He closed his eyes and imagined the blissful quiet.

The dragon at his door shifted slightly, her claws making little scraping sounds to remind him she was there. What was she waiting for? Permission to give him a message? Or was she waiting for him to say her name — and if he didn't, would she go scurrying back to the queen to report that he had failed again?

Perhaps he should enchant a talisman to whisper in his ear whenever he needed to know something. Another tempting idea, but strictly against the rules of IceWing animus magic.

Animus dragons are so rare; appreciate your gift and respect the limits the tribe has set. Never use your power frivolously. Never use it for yourself. This power is extremely dangerous. The tribe's rules are there to protect you. Only the IceWings have figured out how to use animus magic safely.

Save it all for your gifting ceremony. Use it only once in your life, to create a glorious gift to benefit the whole tribe, and then never again; that is the only way to be safe.

Arctic shifted his shoulders, feeling stuck inside his scales. Rules, rules, and more rules: that was the IceWing way of life. Every direction he turned, every thought he had, was restricted by rules and limits and judgmental faces, particularly his mother's. The rules about animus magic were just one more way to keep him trapped under her claws.

"What is it?" he barked at the strange dragon. Annoyed face, try that. As if he were very busy and she'd interrupted him and that was why he was skipping the usual politic rituals. He *was* very busy, actually. The gifting ceremony was only three weeks away. It was bad enough that his mother had dragged him here, to their southernmost palace, near the ocean and the border with the Kingdom of Sand. She'd promised to leave him alone to work while she conducted whatever vital royal business required her presence. Everyone should know better than to disturb him right now.

The messenger looked disappointed. Maybe he really was supposed to know who she was. "Your mother sent me to tell you that the NightWing delegation has arrived."

Aaarrrrgh. Not another boring diplomatic meeting.

"I can't possibly be expected to attend them," he said, waving his claws at the translucent walls of his room. "I only have three more weeks to prepare."

"Well," said the other IceWing, "she did mention that . . ."

"But she doesn't care," he finished when she trailed off.

The poor dragon looked profoundly uncomfortable, caught between a prince who outranked her and a queen who outranked everyone. Arctic sighed.

"Very well," he said, sweeping shards of ice aside with his tail. "I'm coming."

She stepped back with relief, and he realized that

the silver chain around her neck had only one circle on it. Uh-oh. That meant she was ranked in the First Circle — how could he have forgotten a First Circle IceWing? First and Second Circle dragons usually lived in the queen's ice palace alongside the royal family, and he was sure he'd memorized them all.

Except for the nobles who lived in the outer three palaces . . .

"Snowflake," he blurted. He really was an idiot. This was the one his mother had chosen for him to marry. Respectable family, loyal, likely to have a daughter who could replace Queen Diamond one day, since he had no sisters or aunts who might try for the throne. Snowflake was probably the real reason he'd been dragged on this trip.

"Yes," she said, dipping her head. She was pretty in that boring, glassy way his mother liked, but he had gotten absolutely no sense of her personality at their one prior meeting. He was a little afraid she might not have one.

"Uh," he said, following her down the frozen hall. *There must be something we can talk about.* "Have you ever seen a NightWing before?"

"Only the one who came to the wall a few months ago to request this meeting."

"Do you know what they're here for?"

She shook her head. So. That was apparently the end of that conversation.

Ooo, how about an animus-touched object that can make any dragon interesting. Skies above, now that would be useful.

Don't waste your gift! his mother's voice echoed in his head. *Blah blah blah! Careful consideration! Months of planning!*

Sometimes he got a strong feeling that she regretted her own animus gift to the tribe: the gift of healing, which was a set of narwhal horns that could heal frostbreath injuries. It helped when young IceWings played too roughly or when fights broke out within the tribe . . . but it certainly would be a much more useful gift if the horns could heal *any* injuries. He bet Queen Diamond wished she could reach back through time and fix *that* mistake.

"What would you give the tribe?" he asked Snowflake. "If you were an animus, I mean, and had to come up with a gift?"

"Oh," she said, fidgeting her wings in little flippy waves. "I don't know."

"Well, think about it," he said. "I'd really like to know."

"All right," she said. They kept walking through the halls of the palace, which were smaller and more cramped than the ones at home, with odd little mismatched ice carvings everywhere — here a polar bear, there a wolf, there a screaming scavenger, here a lumpy owl. There was no consistency, no sense of an artistic vision, and everything was too close to him. It made Arctic want to smash through the walls just so he could see the sky.

About a minute later, Snowflake said, "Sorry, I can't think of anything."

Arctic couldn't hide the irritation that flashed across his face. "*Really* think about it," he said. "Tell me tomorrow, or whenever you come up with something."

She gave him a look that, to his surprise, was nearly as irritated as his own. "Seems like kind of a waste of my time," she said. "Unless you're having trouble coming up with an idea for yours."

"No, no," he said quickly. "Of course I already have a plan." *Well, Mother has a plan. Which is why I am trying to come up with a better one.*

She didn't ask what it was. Instead she stopped at one of the flight ledges and nodded down at the dome below them. In the gathering dusk, it glowed from within like firelit marble, covering most of the plain between the palace and the ocean. Snow dusted the outside and the ground all around it; more crystalline flakes were falling softly from the sky.

The ocean itself was gouged with streaks of orange and gold as the sun set on the distant western horizon. Dragon wings sliced the air like darting bats as hunters dove to catch dinner in the sea for the welcome banquet tonight.

Arctic and Snowflake flew down to the entrance of the guest dome. Inside, he knew, it would be warmer than he liked, heated by the bodies of the fire-breathing NightWings and also by the gift of diplomacy. (*Created by an animus named Penguin about fifty years ago,* chatted his overstuffed brain. He had studied every animus gift in careful detail, trying to come up with something new and original for his own. Which was perhaps why he didn't have room in his brain for the faces of dragons he barely knew.)

The dome itself was not an animus gift, though; these blocks of ice had been carved by ordinary IceWing talons. It must have taken ages, and he wasn't entirely convinced that it wouldn't all melt on top of some fire-breathing guests one day.

Maybe I could improve the dome as my gift, he thought. *An indestructible welcome dome for any allies or guests from other tribes.* He dismissed the thought almost as soon as he had it. It was derivative and not nearly as impressive as he wanted it to be. He wanted his gift to be one that IceWings would marvel about for centuries after he was gone — something like Frostbite's gift of light.

They landed with a crunch on the snow, but just as they were about to enter the tunnel into the dome, a dragon came charging out.

"Sorry!" she cried breathlessly as she narrowly avoided knocking them over. "I just needed to be outside for a moment. *Look* at that sunset! Great kingdoms, it is freezing out here! I might literally die! But obviously I can't go back inside and miss this sunset. I can handle a little cold, right? If I just . . . keep . . . moving . . ." She began stamping furiously in a circle around them, whacking herself with her wings.

She was a NightWing — the first NightWing Arctic had ever seen. He'd known she would be black, but he hadn't expected the underscales of dark green on her chest or the silver scales that glittered here and there across the underside of her wings. Her eyes, too, seemed a little closer to dark green than to black, and they caught his without any fear. Her wings snapped with energy and he felt his own wings responding, lifting as though he might suddenly take off and touch the moons.

"I'll meet you inside," he said to Snowflake.

She paused, giving the NightWing a disapproving look.

"You can tell my mother I'm coming," he suggested. "Better hurry. She doesn't like to wait."

Snowflake's forehead wrinkled into that irritated expression again, and she turned to whisk down the tunnel without even a bow or ritual farewell.

I suppose that's what I deserve, he thought, *since I didn't give her the greeting her rank requires.* He stared after her for a moment, trying to imagine what it would be like to be married to Snowflake. *Maybe she does have a personality: repressed fury. Or maybe she's as unexcited about this match as I am. I'm not sure how to improve that situation. I mean, I am a prince; if she marries me, she could hatch the next queen. What more could she want?*

"Who stuck an icicle up *her* snout?" asked the NightWing. She started jumping up and down in place, grinning at him.

"I'm afraid that was me, probably," he said. "It took me far too long to remember her name."

"So?" said the black dragon. "I forget names all the time."

"Well, I'm not supposed to forget anyone's," he said. "Also, we're kind of engaged to be married."

The NightWing started laughing so hard she had to sit down, which immediately made her leap up again with a yelp, shaking snow off her tail.

"Are you all right?" he asked.

"Just c-c-cold," she said, stamping her feet again. "All right, I'm on her side. That's pretty terrible. You're the worst."

"I'm not the worst!" he protested. "We've only met once! I barely know her! Also, she is extremely unmemorable!"

"Seriously the worst!" she cried, laughing again. "That poor dragon! I am completely telling her not to marry you. I pity whoever gets tricked into that. You'll be like, 'Happy fortieth anniversary . . . what's your name again?' and she'll be all, 'It's our FIFTIETH, you slime weasel, and my name is you're sleeping on an iceberg tonight.'"

"I promise I would remember that name," he said. "Sticks in the brain a bit better than Snowflake."

"And what's your name?" she asked. "Or I can keep calling you slime weasel, although I suspect that might get me kicked off the peacekeeping committee."

"My name is Arctic. Prince Arctic."

"Oh, *fancy*," she said. "I guess I shouldn't bother telling you mine, since you'll forget it in the next five minutes anyway."

"I promise I won't," he protested.

"Oh, you only forget your girlfriends' names?" she joked. "Or future family members?"

"I remember any dragon who seems likely to change my life," he said.

"That's not me!" she cried, looking genuinely startled. "I'm under strict orders not to do any damage or break any ice palaces or corrupt any IceWings or change any lives. Then again, I'm pretty sure I've never followed an order in my life, so . . . you know, watch your back, ice palaces."

Never followed an order in her life! Arctic blinked at her, enchanted and mystified. How was that possible? Life was nothing but a series of orders; if you didn't follow them, wouldn't you get lost or drop to the bottom of the rankings or be thrown out of your tribe? *Imagine disobeying an order — any order. Where would I even start?*

"AAAAAAAH, why is it SO COLD?" The NightWing leaped into the air and started doing vigorous somersaults.

"Because this is the Ice Kingdom," he said, standing back out of her way. "It's true, though, our climate is one of our best-guarded secrets."

"Oh, he's a wise guy, too," she said, righting herself and landing again. "Do you have any *useful* skills, or maybe an extra one of those magic bracelets that keeps your guests from freezing?"

"That's the gift of diplomacy," he said. "It keeps our guests warm and helps them travel safely over the Great Ice Cliff. The tribe only has three bracelets — are there more than three of you?" he asked, surprised.

"I'm the fourth," she said. "My mother and I are sharing her bracelet; there was some back and forth silliness to get over your cliff. I *probably* should have asked for it before I came outside."

"We could go inside," he said reluctantly. Inside there would be other dragons, infinitely more boring dragons, not to mention his mother, and probably a new set of rules about appeasing Snowflake, staying away from NightWings, and generally acting more like an obedient puddle. "Or we could stay to watch the rest of the sunset . . ."

"The sunset is great," she said, "but honestly I had to come out here because my mother is driving me *crazy*."

He couldn't control the smile that split his face like ice cracking. It seemed possible that he would never be able to stop smiling at her. He'd never heard an IceWing say anything like that about his or her parents; it was beyond forbidden to complain or talk back or criticize your elders in any fashion.

"Please tell me *all* about it," he said.

"Oh, she's always lecturing me about how I ruin everything. Foeslayer, why are the scrolls shelved in the wrong places again? Foeslayer, you smiled at the wrong dragons this morning! Foeslayer, the queen will never want you on her council if you insist on having opinions all the time. Foeslayer, I'm bringing you on this mission because I don't trust you if I leave you behind, but if you say *one word to any IceWing*, I will mount your head on a spike in the throne room." She snapped her mouth shut as if she'd just understood that last instruction, then gave Arctic a rueful look. "Um . . . oops."

"Aha," he said, with a thrill like the first time he'd touched fire. "I have cleverly deduced that your name is Foeslayer."

"Oh no," she said. "That's just how my mother · starts all her sentences."

He laughed and she smiled and he thought that perhaps nothing would ever be boring or frustrating again as long as he was near her.

"So really," she said, "no secret extra magic bracelets? Or a blanket or anything?"

"Sorry," Arctic said, wishing he could offer his own wings for warmth — but his scales were as cold as the snow underfoot and would only make things worse.

She sighed. "Then I guess I do have to go back inside."

"Wait," he said. He didn't stop to think about it. It was wrong, worse than wrong: a broken rule, a betrayal of his entire tribe, but next to this shining dragon he didn't care. He'd do anything for another few minutes with her.

He unclipped the diamond earring from his ear, held it between his talons, and said softly, "I enchant this earring to keep the dragon wearing it warm no matter the temperature . . . and to keep her safe no matter the danger."

Her dark green eyes were wide with disbelief as he leaned over and gently curled the earring around her ear. His talons lingered there for a moment, brushing against the smooth warmth of her long, dark neck. The shivering in her scales slowed to a stop, and she cautiously held out her wings to the cold air.

"Whoa. That — that *worked*," she said. "So the rumors are true — your tribe *does* have magic."

"Only a few of us," he said. "And so does yours, doesn't it?"

"Only a few of us," she echoed, "and not like that. I don't have anything, for instance. You just — can you enchant anything? To do anything?"

"Animus power," he said, taking a step closer to her. "That's how it works."

"Then why don't the IceWings rule the entire continent?" she asked, her tail skipping nervously over the snowy ground. "You don't even need this alliance. You could destroy the SkyWings easily, couldn't you?"

He shook his head. "The tribe has strict rules. We're only allowed to use our power once in a lifetime."

Foeslayer's talon flew to the earring and she stared at him, shocked into stillness for the first time.

"Well," he said with a shrug, "perhaps I'm not much of a rule follower either." He felt another thrill at the idea of being that dragon, of being seen that way by *this* dragon. He reached out tentatively and brushed her wing with his. She didn't pull away.

"Why?" Foeslayer whispered.

"It's these old legends we have," Arctic said, "warning us of the dangers of animus magic — use it too much, you lose your soul, some mystical mumbo jumbo like that, which probably isn't even true. But once there's a law set down in the Ice Kingdom, everyone better follow it with no questions asked." He decided not to mention the ancient stories of animus dragons gone mad.

"No," Foeslayer said, touching the earring again. "Why did you do this — for me?" She wrinkled her snout, half teasing, half serious. "Aren't you worried about your soul?"

"Not anymore," he said. "It's yours now . . . if you want it."

Glittering petals of snow fell softly on her black wings, melting into her heat. Foeslayer hesitated, then reached out and took one of Arctic's talons in hers.

This is a bad idea, whispered Arctic's conscience. *The very worst. Neither of our tribes would forgive us. Mother will never allow it.*

All the more reason. I won't let the queen crush my entire life between her claws.

It's my life, my magic, and my heart.

"I'm going to say something really sappy," Foeslayer warned him.

"More sappy than what I just said?" he asked. "I'd like to see you try."

"I just — I have this strange feeling," Foeslayer said, looking into his eyes, "that the world is about to change forever."

DISCOVER THE #1 *NEW YORK TIMES* BESTSELLING SERIES!

◄ THE DRAGONET PROPHECY ►

◄ THE JADE MOUNTAIN PROPHECY ►

◄ THE LOST CONTINENT PROPHECY ►   ## ◄ LEGENDS ►

◄ GRAPHIC NOVELS ►